"Miss Lane."

She paused and looked back at him, hoping he couldn't see the sudden panic she'd been unable to suppress.

"I didn't mean to make you nervous."

She forced a smile to her lips. "It's just first-day-on-the-job jitters, that's all," Dani said. "I'll be fine in the morning."

He took a step toward her. "If there's anything you need . . ." The cat jumped from his arms to the floor, and Dani shrieked, stepping back hurriedly as the animal dashed past her on its way toward the foyer.

She looked back at Anton and found him frowning. "Sorry, it . . . startled me."

"Are you certain it was the cat who frightened you, Miss Lane"—he smiled as the molten steel of his eyes burned into hers—"and not me?"

WHAT ARE *LOVESWEPT* ROMANCES?

They are stories of true romance and touching emotion. We believe those two very important ingredients are constants in our highly sensual and very believable stories in the LOVESWEPT line. Our goal is to give you, the reader, stories of consistently high quality that may sometimes make you laugh, sometimes make you cry, but are always fresh and creative and contain many delightful surprises within their pages.

Most romance fans read an enormous number of books. Those they truly love, they keep. Others may be traded with friends and soon forgotten. We hope that each LOVESWEPT romance will be a treasure—a "keeper." We will always try to publish

LOVE STORIES YOU'LL NEVER FORGET
BY AUTHORS YOU'LL ALWAYS REMEMBER

The Editors

WHEN NIGHT FALLS

CHERYLN BIGGS

BANTAM BOOKS
NEW YORK · TORONTO · LONDON · SYDNEY · AUCKLAND

WHEN NIGHT FALLS
A Bantam Book / November 1996

ISBN 0-553-44552-9

Published simultaneously in the United States and Canada

*Bantam Books are published by Bantam Books, a division of Bantam Dou-
bleday Dell Publishing Group, Inc. Its trademark, consisting of the words
"Bantam Books" and the portrayal of a rooster, is Registered in U.S.
Patent and Trademark Office and in other countries. Marca Registrada.
Bantam Books, 1540 Broadway, New York, New York 10036.*

PRINTED IN THE UNITED STATES OF AMERICA
OPM   0 9 8 7 6 5 4 3 2 1

This book is dedicated to Jack, my very own dark, seductive lover, and keeper of the animals. I love you.

Dear Reader,

Dark and mysterious. Seductive and irresistible. Brave and compassionate.

What better words to describe Batman? A man who wore two faces, who presented himself to the outside world as exactly what they saw, while allowing only a special few to see his "secret" face—his inner self.

Batman was my inspiration for the type of hero I wanted to create for WHEN NIGHT FALLS. A hero who had survived a soul-wrenching tragedy and learned to deal with the consequences it forced upon his heart, a man who was strong and hard, who could hold his own in the ruthless world of business and high finance, yet at other times be so sensitive and caring that it could make a woman cry.

That type of man needs a special atmosphere. So Anton Reichard has his dark and secluded, but breathtakingly beautiful New Orleans plantation. And he has Dani Coroneaux, a staunchly independent newspaper journalist who has made it her mission to unmask the man behind the wealth, power, and possible scandal . . . the man many in Louisiana have come to hate and fear.

Cheryln Biggs

PROLOGUE

The breath caught in her throat.

He stood across the room from her, his dark hair slightly disheveled, one ebony lock dangling onto his forehead, accentuating the roguish gleam that sparked from blue eyes as infinite as the fog that sometimes covered the French Quarter on a cold winter's night. The white shirt he wore clung to him, each seam and thread molding to sculpted muscles and well-honed planes, the top four buttons, undone, giving a view of a sliver of golden skin sprinkled with a matting of dark, silky hairs.

As if brought aware of her presence by a sixth sense, he turned slowly and looked her way. Dani's heart nearly stopped its erratic beating as his eyes slowly, daringly, seduced the very clothes from her body, his gaze disrobing her every bit as much as if he'd reached out and done so with his hands.

An unfamiliar feeling, like delicious anticipation, caressed her senses. She shivered and watched him walk toward her, his gaze, hooded and heavy with passion, raking over her, teasing her own building desire and turning her flesh to a blanket of scorching heat.

An aura of darkness swirled around him, challenging, defying anyone to come close, to brave the danger that tenebrous unknown promised. The sense of his domination and feral quality excited her, and it was a feeling that was both alien and pleasurable, that fascinated and scared her. She felt the heat of his body reach out to touch her flesh as he stopped before her. The heady sensation that she was about to be conquered, like an innocent twelfth-century virgin, assailed her as he grasped her shoulders within the cups of his strong hands and crushed his mouth to hers, claiming her for his own with a kiss that left her unable to think.

In direct contrast to the near unyielding independence of her nature, she reveled in his assault, in his victory over her emotions.

His mouth was like a touch of volcanic lava to her skin, traveling slowly from her parted lips to the hollow of her cheek, down the long column of her neck, over the delicate curve of her shoulder—sealing his brand upon her for all time, body and soul. She'd been kissed before, loved before, but this man's kiss, this man's touch, was like none she had ever experienced. His was the kiss of an angel, the touch of the devil, turning her blood to fire and vanquishing her inhibitions and reservations.

She felt his hands brush aside the thin fabric of her blouse and release the small hook at the front of her lacy brassiere, baring her breasts to him. Dani arched toward him, needing, pleading for his touch, and slipped her hands through the dark, rich waves of his hair as he bent to take her nipple into his mouth.

Need, pleasure, and hungry desire exploded within every cell of her body, and every new emotion that had awakened in her with the sensation was imprinted with his name.

Crushing her to him with an arm around her waist, his other hand moved down over the curve of her hip, his touch as light as the brush of a feather, as arousing as the caress of hot velvet against tender flesh. His hand slipped under her skirt and slid slowly, teasingly, up her inner thigh.

Dani groaned softly. The ecstasy of his touch, the growing need within her to know more of it, was almost beyond what she could bear.

The sound of a fist smashing against wood shattered the haze of passion that had enveloped Dani. The shrill voice that followed it brought her jerkingly and somewhat uncomprehendingly, back to reality. "Dani? Dani, are you here?"

Bolting upright in bed, her heart hammering madly, pulse racing, Dani looked around the room, disoriented, breasts heaving as she sucked in a ragged breath. Her bedroom. Recognition came slowly, quickly, her thoughts, memories, a jumble, reality and dream still intertwined as she wavered between wakefulness and sleep.

"Dani?" Another loud knock. "Dani?"

She kicked at the sheets tangled about her bare legs, grabbed her robe from the chair beside the bed, and dashed to the front door. Half of her mind was painfully alert to her surroundings, the time, what was happening. The other half was still lost within the effects of her dream, still struggling to emerge from the hazy fantasy her imagination had drawn her into as she'd slept, and to which she'd reacted, physically, much more strongly than she wanted to acknowledge.

Dani threw open the door and stared at the red-haired pixie who stood on the opposite side of the threshold. "Kate," Dani muttered. Her ride to work. She was late. She'd slept right through her alarm. Dani shook her head and wiped a hand over her face, as if to clear her thoughts and erase the heaviness of sleep that still had her in its grip. "Jeez, I, uh, overslept. Sorry. Go on without me."

"You don't look too good, Dani," Kate said. "You're flushed." Her freckled nose wrinkled as she frowned. "Are you sick? Want me to run to the drugstore and get you some aspirin or something?"

"No, I'm fine." Dani pushed a long lock of dark hair from her face, then made a shooing motion toward Kate with her hand. "Go on to work before you're late. Tell Stan I'll be there soon."

"Are you sure?"

"Yes. I'm fine, really. Now go. I'll be in the office shortly." She shut the door and practically collapsed against it, leaning her forehead into the hard wood. She stayed that way until her heartbeat returned to normal and her pulse slowed to a comfortable pace.

How ridiculous could a person's dreams get?

She pushed away from the door, deciding she didn't really want an answer to that question, and walked back into her bedroom. The king-size bed, with its multishelved headboard and built-in nightstands, was a jumble of rumpled sheets, and scattered atop them, as well as all over the floor, were dozens of newspaper articles she had photocopied from the paper's morgue over the past few weeks. She'd been going over them again before she'd fallen asleep.

Dani approached the bed and looked down at the array of articles. Several were accompanied by pictures of Anton Reichard. One in particular caught her gaze. It had a caption beneath the picture, stating that it had been taken after a party at the New Orleans Country Club five years before. Anton stood facing the photographer, though obviously not aware of him. His dark hair was slightly disheveled, one ebony lock dangling onto his forehead, accentuating the roguish gleam that sparked from eyes as infinite as the fog that sometimes covered the French Quarter on a cold winter's night. The shirt he wore clung to him, each seam and thread molding to sculpted muscles and well-honed planes, the top four buttons, undone, giving a view of a sliver of skin sprinkled with a matting of dark, silky hairs.

ONE

Anton Reichard moved silently through the dark rooms of Bayou Noir, his steps guided by years of familiarity with his surroundings. He ignored the lightninglike jolts of pain that shot through his right leg. The injury was long healed, but the doctors had said he'd have pain if he put too much strain on it, as he'd done that day. Usually, even when in pain, he could control the limp by sheer willpower, conceal it from the sight of others, but at night, when alone, he didn't bother.

Most of the drapes in the house had been drawn, but pale moonlight flowed into the foyer through the beveled fanlight window set over the entry door. The soft glow shone upon the oak balustrade that curled its way upstairs, touched the rich wood of the grandfather clock that had been sitting in the same spot of the foyer since the house had been built over a hundred and eighty years before, and finally crept across the foyer's black-and-white-checkered marble floor to warm the edge of the Aubusson rug in the front parlor.

He left the light behind and walked through the

darkness to his study, moving instinctively around the large desk that dominated the room. But he didn't settle into the wing-backed leather chair set behind it. There was no reason to sit, no use in trying to relax. His nerves were too on edge to allow him that comfort. He turned on the small Tiffany lamp that sat on his desk. The moment the faint light filtered through the lamp's multicolored stained glass shade, Anton's gaze shifted to the portrait that hung over the fireplace. His family was gone now, and it was all his fault.

A deep sigh rattled through his body, intensifying the loneliness and guilt that had taken up residence within him ever since the accident. Sometimes when he looked at the portrait of his parents and sister, Sherry, he felt as if they were looking down on him in forgiveness, letting him know, somehow, that they realized it hadn't been his fault, that he would give anything to be able to turn back the clock and change what had happened. Other times he felt as if they were damning him, cursing every breath he took, enjoying the agony that lived in his heart and reminded him every day, every minute, of what he'd done. He had been the one flying the plane, he could almost hear them whisper at times. He had been the one so much in a hurry to leave Dallas, the one to ignore the storm warnings, and yet he was the one who was alive—while they were dead.

Turning away from the portrait he had come to both love and dread looking at, Anton turned off the lamp and stared into the darkness. It was usually more comforting there, in the warmth of the shadows, but not tonight. He moved to the window and, frustrated beyond reason without even knowing why, slashed out at the blue damask drape, tossing the heavy fabric aside. He stared out at the night with unseeing eyes. In a movement that was unconscious habit, but only one of several he'd developed since the accident, he ran a hand through his hair, long fingers sliding easily through waves of cimmerian darkness that shone softly beneath the wan touch of the night's light.

Exhaustion weighed heavy on his body, but he knew there was no reason to return to his bed. He wouldn't be able to sleep. It was the same every night. A few hours of fitful slumber while, against his will, the barriers he'd built to keep out the memories crumbled and his traitorous mind remembered what he so desperately wanted to forget, replaying the events of that day over and over.

While he tossed and turned, trying to find some peaceful sleep, some shred of rest, yet at the same time trying to wake from the quagmire of torment and failing, his mind would force him, with torturous clarity, to relive that one horrible moment when he'd lost control of the plane, and his life had changed forever.

He always woke up with a start, a scream threatening to strangle him as it struggled to break from his throat, tears filling his eyes, his heart seized by a fear deeper and more piercing than any he'd ever known. Then, with slamming force, the truth would crash back down upon him, cruelly reminding him that the images he'd just endured weren't merely a dream, or even a horrible nightmare, but memories of reality.

Within seconds, a sense of loss, of utter aloneness and despair, would envelop him, and the rest of the night he'd wander aimlessly through the house, trying to calm his jangled nerves, understand why he had been spared, and forget how badly he'd failed. It had been the same every night for three years, and he had no doubt it would be the same every night for the rest of his life.

But it was no more than he deserved.

"You want to do what?"

Dani smiled at her boss. "Come on, Stan, don't look at me as if I'd just said I wanted to take a swim with a dozen hungry gators."

"At least *that's* possible, Coroneaux."

Clenched fists shot up and slammed down on her hips. "And you think getting a story on Anton Reichard is not?"

He snorted. "Hardly. The way I understand it, no one's even seen the guy since a few months after the accident, except his secretary, housekeeper, and lawyers." Stan Gates rose, ran a hand over his bald pate as if pushing back hair that was no longer there, and began to pace the narrow space of floor behind his desk.

Dani waited nervously. She'd been a junior investigative reporter in Shreveport for two years, but she had only come to work for the *Picayune* newspaper in New Orleans three weeks earlier. Stan hadn't given her an assignment yet, just had her helping others in order to familiarize herself with the *Picayune*'s staff and ways, but his not assigning her a story didn't matter because she'd come there knowing exactly what she wanted to investigate. Now all she had to do was talk him into it.

Memory of her dream about Anton Reichard suddenly invaded her thoughts, and Dani shivered, though whether the reaction was due to the dream's erotic nature or the fact that she'd had the dream at all, she wasn't sure. It wasn't something she planned to worry about, however. After all, it had been only a dream. And a ridiculous one at that.

Reporters from every newspaper, magazine, and television station in the state had tried to get an interview with Reichard after the accident that had killed his parents and sister and had ultimately turned him into a recluse. No one had succeeded in nearly three years—not even Dani's father, and he was considered one of the best investigative journalists in the country. She felt a spurt of satisfaction at the fact that her father had tried to get to Reichard and failed. That didn't happen to Harlen Coroneaux very often.

Interest in Reichard had eventually waned, but in the last few months he'd recaptured the media's attentions, and their efforts to get to him had been renewed. The third anniversary of the plane crash was approaching, which would make a touching human-interest piece. But even more newsworthy was a financial interest he now had in—or more correctly, was threatening to pull out of—one of the largest casino ventures being built in New Orleans. The project was behind schedule and running over budget and, for all intents and purposes, looked on the verge of financial ruin. If that happened, and it most certainly would if Reichard pulled out, it would destroy a number of smaller businessmen, contractors, and city officials who had invested time and money in the venture. That could prove to be one of the most scandalous stories of the year . . . if it happened . . . and if a reporter was able to get close enough to Reichard to get the inside details.

Dani had wanted to do a story on Anton Reichard ever since he'd gone into seclusion, but the *Shreveport*

Daily News editor had always said no. He didn't have any interest in a billionaire recluse, Louisiana native or not. But now Dani was working in New Orleans, Reichard's hometown, and his financial maneuverings were threatening a major disaster for the city. The timing and the angle were perfect.

Stan shook his head, drawing Dani's attention back to the moment. "It won't work, Dani. The man just won't cooperate. We've had other reporters try to get to Reichard, and no one's ever succeeded."

Dani smiled. "I can." As far as she knew not one other reporter had picked up on what had happened the other day, not even Stan. It could be a golden opportunity, and if her plan worked, it would get her a story that could take her career straight to the top. Then her father wouldn't be able to dismiss her so easily.

Anton Reichard's story was her key to success. Just the thought of the man, however, threatened to bring memory of the dream dancing back through her mind. She shrugged it aside. Getting the story on him could put her career where she wanted it to be. *That* was why he was on her mind, *that* was why she could think of nothing else, and *that* was why he'd invaded her dreams. She'd done a lot of research on him over the past three years, preparing for the day she could write his story. The tragedy that had struck his family, his hiding himself away from the world, becoming almost a completely different person, doubling his family's holdings while cutting off all their previous charitable contributions, never going anywhere, never enjoying his financial successes—it all fascinated her.

She had waited for almost three years for the right

opportunity to present itself, for the right time to do his story, and now it was here . . . she hoped.

"How long's it been since Reichard's plane accident, Coroneaux?" Stan said. His gruff voice, and the question, jerked her attention back to their conversation just as her mind had once again begun to conjure up memory of the dream that had turned her body hungry with desire.

She pulled the collar of her blouse away from her neck. "Three years," Dani answered, her voice ragged as it struggled past a throat suddenly gone as dry as the city streets before a summer shower.

"Okay, let's say I do give you the go-ahead on this thing, how would you get to him? Judging from the work you did up in Shreveport, you're a damned good reporter and on your way to being even better. That's why I hired you. But Reichard never leaves his plantation, and does all of his business dealings through his secretary or his—"

"She died."

Stan stopped pacing and turned to stare at her. Sunlight shone through the windows at his side and fell on his face, highlighting its craggy lines and causing shadows to delve within his heavy wrinkles, accentuating them. He frowned, and his brow suddenly resembled a road map of converging freeways. "She died," he repeated, a look of puzzlement in his eyes.

Dani nodded and sat down in the seat opposite Stan's desk. "The service is tomorrow."

"So, what?"

"I'm going to apply for her job."

"I've got a better idea," Stan said. "And one that will

work." He picked up a memo from his "in" basket. "There's been some rumors floating around about a strike by the local garbage workers' union. That happened several years ago during Mardi Gras and had the whole city in an uproar. Go talk to the union leaders, see what they're thinking, what they want."

"Oh, come on, Stan." Dani popped back onto her feet, too agitated to remain seated or worry that she might be putting her new job in jeopardy. "Anybody can go talk to those guys. Anyway, when you hired me you promised that I could pick some of my own stories." She glared at him. "And a garbage workers' strike is not my idea of investigative journalism. Reichard's story could be front-page stuff. Think about it: New Orleans's own Howard Hughes. Anton Reichard—rich, reclusive, and eccentric." She began to move around the room. "He used to be one of the most sought-after bachelors in the country. In the society pages of half a dozen newspapers almost every day. He dated some of the world's most beautiful women."

"Yeah, I remember."

"But since a few months after the accident no one has seen him, except the small circle of employees he keeps around himself. He's cut himself off from society, friends, and relatives, staying hidden away twenty-four hours a day every day on his plantation and doing all of his business by phone, fax, or computer. And there's one other thing . . ." She paused, hoping she'd pricked Stan's interest enough for him to snatch at the bait.

He did. "What other thing?"

"Anton Reichard terminated all of his family's charitable contributions, and they were big on that, Stan. Especially Anton's father. He was a real philanthropist. Orphanages, cancer research, hospital wings, city benefits, literacy, you name it, he had probably donated to it."

"So? The son's tight."

Dani shook her head. "Maybe, but I don't think so. It doesn't make sense. He stays sequestered out at that plantation, working, making money, and for what? Where's it going?"

"Into the casino venture."

"No. If he was footing all the expenses there, he wouldn't have partners or the bank involved."

"So what are you saying?" Stan asked.

"I don't know. Yet." Dani tossed her head and dark swirls of ginger-brown hair fanned out across her shoulders. "But there's something there. A story, Stan, a good one. Maybe better than we could imagine, I don't know. But this may be our only opportunity to get it."

He sat back and folded his arms as if barricading himself against her, his eyes narrowed, gaze boring into her. "And you want it before your father goes after it, right?"

"Yes."

Stan nodded. "Okay. But as I asked before, just how do you plan on getting to Reichard if I give the go-ahead for this story?"

She felt a surge of excitement course through her. "I need you to help me construct a cover. I've only been here at the *Picayune* for a few weeks, so it should be easy to conceal that. Shreveport might be a bit harder, but I'm sure my old editor there will cooperate and clear my name out of their personnel files. I figure to use a phony name and social security number, and set up a fake background, blended with a little truth, just in case they pull up something on me. It's always easier to lie when some of the lie is based on truth."

"Sounds feasible so far. What's the background you figure on setting up?"

"Married straight out of business school, husband and child recently died in an auto accident. I'm a widow with excellent schooling and clerical skills but no real work experience, and I need the job."

Stan laughed. "What makes you think someone like Reichard will hire a person with no experience?"

Dani shrugged. "I not only have excellent clerical skills, I'm willing to sequester myself miles from town in order to land the job. I doubt there will be too many applicants willing to do that, and since staying at the plantation six days a week, twenty-four hours a day was required of his last secretary, I'm assuming the situation will be the same for his new hire."

"The line about the dead husband and kid might be a bit much," Stan said somberly. "Too melodramatic."

Dani smiled. "But effective."

The ride to Bayou Noir took thirty minutes. It should have taken forty-five, but Anton Reichard's personal attorney liked to drive at death-defying speeds. Snaking two-lane highways and blind curves obviously were nothing more than a challenge to him. Dani tried for the hundredth time since getting into Carter Tyrene's little red sports car to convince herself it wasn't her day to die. He took another curve. She grabbed the door grip and was on number one hundred and one when the car slowed and swerved from the highway onto a narrow drive.

Dani sighed in relief and sagged against the back of the seat.

Sprawling ancient oak trees lined both sides of the long entry, their twisted and gnarled branches, heavily draped with thick curtains of gray Spanish moss, meeting overhead to create a tunnel. Sunlight fell through this trellis of living growth here and there in sparse patches, leaving the ground checkered by light and shadow.

"Well, here we are," Carter announced needlessly.

Dani glanced at the blond Adonis who was not only Reichard's personal attorney, but also his best friend, and tried to squelch the nervousness that seized her at his words. She was finally going to meet Anton Reichard, and if she could get past this last interview, she would get the story that might catapult her career into the big time.

And make her father realize she could do more than help her mother in the kitchen, Dani thought sullenly.

The car rolled around a curve in the drive, and Reichard's plantation house came into view. The pictures Dani had seen in magazines did not do it justice. Bayou Noir was spectacular, its architecture of wide galleries, slender columns, and shutter-framed windows an ingenious blend of Caribbean elegance and Southern antebellum majesty.

Carter pulled his car to a stop directly before a slate walkway that led to the house, then hurried around the low-slung vehicle to help her out with a flourish, more as if he were delivering a princess to the castle rather than a job applicant to an interview.

Dani walked beside him toward the house, but before she had taken more than a step across the wide gallery, the entry door swung quietly open. A sense of foreboding assailed her, and she hesitated, suddenly not so certain she wanted to walk through the yawning entrance beyond which she could see nothing but darkness.

But Carter Tyrene's hand at her elbow urged her forward.

As they approached the entry a woman of astounding and exotic beauty stepped out from behind the door, startling Dani with her sudden and eerily silent appearance.

"Sanitee, good afternoon," Carter said.

The housekeeper nodded but remained reticent, her green eyes meeting Dani's coolly, then gliding over her in blatant assessment.

Sanitee. Dani felt an odd sense of unease at the woman's scrutiny. Some of the stories she'd read about Anton Reichard, especially those concerning the family's accident, had mentioned his housekeeper, hinting that some believed she was descended from a long line of voodoo queens and had unusual powers. One article had gone so far as to claim that she'd predicted the deaths of Anton's parents and sister . . . as well as the fact that they would die by his hand.

And in a way they had, Dani realized with a shudder.

"This is Miss Danielle Lane, Sanitee," Carter said, by way of introduction. "The young lady who is interviewing with Anton today."

Danielle forced a smile to her lips. She had chosen the fake last name on a whim, taking it from one of the most celebrated of fictional females, newspaper reporter Lois Lane.

Sanitee reached out and took one of Dani's hands in hers. "Welcome to Bayou Noir, Miss Lane." A lilting accent that Dani was hard put to identify caressed each of the woman's words, but her tone, like both her hands and eyes, held no warmth.

Dani forced herself to smile and tried to pull her hand back, but Sanitee held tight. "You are nervous," she said softly, looking deeply into Dani's eyes. "But not about the position here."

Dani stared at the woman, not certain what to say.

"You are nervous about Anton," Sanitee continued. "And your past. That he will not approve of it." She released Dani's hand and stepped back. "Please, come in." She waved them past her with a sweep of an arm whose flesh was the color of café au lait, and as she did, at least a dozen gold bracelets jangled upon her wrist.

Dani felt a shiver of unease ripple its way up her spine. Had the woman seen the fake résumé she'd submitted to Carter Tyrene and was she referring to her supposed lack of clerical experience? Or was Sanitee psychic, as the rumors claimed, and had subtly notified Dani that she knew the truth about her? That they all knew.

The thought did nothing for her nerves, which were already frazzled.

Anton Reichard stepped away from the sheer, lace-covered window in his study. Danielle Lane was nothing like he'd expected. That thought had struck him the moment she'd emerged from the car—sleek, sensual, moving with a fluidity of grace that instantly unnerved him.

Carter had described her to him, told him everything about her, but in spite of that, Anton had formed an image that was nothing like the woman he had watched walk across the gallery of his home.

He'd wanted her to be plain, older, subdued. She was none of those, and he wasn't certain he was sorry.

"Sanitee," Carter said, "I noticed Mr. Pellichet's car in the drive."

"Yes, he is waiting for Miss Lane in the parlor."

Dani frowned and turned her gaze to Carter Tyrene's. "Mr. Pellichet?"

"I'm sorry," Carter said hurriedly, "I forgot to tell you, Floyd is the attorney who handles Anton's special, somewhat newer, interests. He requested a word with you before you interviewed with Anton. It shouldn't take but a minute." He smiled apologetically, though Dani had the distinct impression that Carter Tyrene hadn't forgotten a thing. It was a test, and she decided to give one of her own.

"Newer interest, like the casino venture?" Dani asked.

Carter frowned and looked at her for a long second before answering. "Yes, the casino venture." He motioned her toward a room off the unlit foyer. "Shall we?"

Dani preceded him into the parlor.

A man with a shock of gray-streaked black hair and a face as angular as any Dani had ever seen, rose from a chair near the fireplace. He held his hand out to her. "It's good to meet you, Miss Lane." His voice filled the room, but it was warm and welcoming rather than intimidating. "Carter has spoken quite highly of your qualifications."

Dani smiled, but the exuberant attorney hadn't quite captured her attention enough to keep her from noticing the tall, dark-haired man disappearing through a doorway at the opposite end of the room.

TWO

Anton Reichard stood beside Carter and stared into the parlor through a one-way mirror. Dani was responding to a comment from Floyd. "You've rechecked her background, Carter?"

"What there is of it, yes. I didn't come up with anything new. As you already know, she has excellent skills, but no work history, which a check on her social security number verifies. She was an orphan, grew up in a convent in Baton Rouge, also verified. The only thing I haven't been able to confirm is her claim of losing her husband and child, though I did document that a couple and a child rented the previous address she gave me. Under her name. I haven't located any recent death certificates for anyone named Lane, or a marriage license, but, then, the way things are today, maybe they weren't really married. Or maybe they were married out of state." He shrugged. "Hell, maybe the husband and kid died out of state while they were on vacation, or maybe Danielle and her husband were separated and he had the kid." Carter sighed in frustration. "There could be a hundred explanations, but those aren't the kinds of questions you normally ask in an interview, Tony, you know?"

Anton frowned and let his gaze move over her again.

"Anyway, there weren't too many other applicants willing to closet themselves out here for twenty-four hours a day, six days a week," Carter added.

The frown pulling at Anton's brow deepened. She had swept her dark brown hair back and secured it in an old-fashioned bun, but it still wasn't enough to suppress the goldish-red highlights that danced throughout the silky strands, nor were the glasses she wore enough to camouflage the midnight blue of her eyes. And they definitely were not enough distraction to keep Anton from noticing the way her nose turned up at the end in a sassy flare, or the sensuously full lips that looked more as if they should be smiling or laughing than prudishly pursed the way she was holding them.

Beneath the staid demeanor she'd affected, it was obvious that Dani Lane was a very attractive woman, and that made Anton more than a little uncomfortable. "She doesn't look like a secretary, Carter," he said, finally.

"Maybe that's because you're used to Amylene, who was seventy-four years old."

Anton's gaze strolled over Dani again, as if reassessing her delicate features, the brown hair that looked as if both the sun and moon had danced within its strands and left their light, and the svelte figure she'd attempted to conceal by draping it with a very plain and simply cut blue linen suit. He turned abruptly to stare at Carter for several long seconds before spinning on his heel and walking across the foyer. "Show her into my study when she's through with Pellichet."

Carter didn't bother to hide the smug smile that tugged at his lips as he watched Anton walk away. He turned toward the parlor door, knocked, and entered. "Floyd, I'm sorry, but Anton would like to see Miss Lane now."

Floyd Pellichet rose and shook Dani's hand, then looked at Carter. "I'll need a minute of your time before I leave, Carter. Some financial details we need to discuss."

Dani saw a wary look pass over Carter's features at Floyd Pellichet's words. "I'll be back in a minute, Floyd." He turned to Dani. "Anton's waiting in . . ."

The slamming of the entry door cut off Carter's words, the loud crash reverberating through the house like a clap of thunder.

"Tony! Dammit, where are you, you damned bastard?"

Dani saw Carter and Floyd stiffen and exchange worried looks, then Carter swore under his breath and hurried toward the foyer. She turned a questioning gaze to Floyd, but when he didn't seem forthcoming with an explanation, she ventured a question. "Is something wrong?"

He smiled, but it seemed a weak effort at best. "Nothing to worry about, I'm sure. Just Jim Knight."

As if to contradict his comment, loud but muffled shouts suddenly echoed through the house.

Floyd snatched his briefcase from a nearby chair. "I'm sorry, Miss Lane, but I really must go. I've several appointments in town and"—he glanced at his watch—"a business meeting."

She watched him leave, then walked into the foyer and stood in front of a huge grandfather clock, as if to admire it. But the beauty of the clock was far from what she really had on her mind. She wanted to hear what was going on behind the tall set of closed doors a few feet away.

"You know damned well that if you pull out now, I'll be ruined."

"You knew the risks of investment when you went into this deal, Jim."

Dani didn't recognize the voices, but she knew that Jim Knight was the name of the man who had been engaged to Anton Reichard's late sister, Sherry.

"You son of a . . ."

"Jim, Jim. . . ." Dani recognized the voice as Carter Tyrene's. "There's really no reason for you to be upset. There are a lot of things to consider before we make a decision about this."

"We?" A harsh, sardonic jeer sliced the air. "Don't fool yourself, Carter, there isn't any 'we' in this decision. Good old Tony looks out for Tony, and the rest of us be damned, or killed. Isn't that right, Tony? Oh wait . . ." he laughed, an ugly, taunting sound that caused Dani to recoil in distaste, "excuse me, but it's *Anton* now, isn't it?"

A long silence followed Jim Knight's spiteful words, and Dani found herself leaning toward the closed door, holding her breath, and waiting for she wasn't sure what.

"Get out, Jim," a low, menacing voice said.

Dani stiffened against the dark threat in both the voice and words, knowing instinctively that it belonged to Anton Reichard.

"Get out before I do something I don't want to do."

"Like kill me, Tony?" Jim Knight taunted. "Sorry, you're too late. I'm a walking dead man. Have been ever since you murdered your sister. All I have left is business, the same as you . . . but quite frankly, I'm not finding it enough to make me forget."

The door suddenly snapped open, and Dani jumped, startled.

A tall man with dark brown hair and amber eyes glimmering with hatred stalked into the foyer, stopped, and spun back to glare into the open doorway. "Don't push me on this, Tony, or you might find out you're not the only one who's capable of murder."

Spinning on his heel, Jim Knight stormed past Dani and out the entry door without so much as giving her a glance.

She didn't know what kind of "investment" Jim had made with Anton Reichard, but from what she'd overheard, Dani figured it was a safe guess that they'd been discussing the casino venture. She made a mental note to get Stan to check on it as soon as possible.

Almost before she finished the thought, Carter walked into the foyer. "Miss Lane, excuse the interruption. One of our associates, um, seemed to be having a small problem this morning." He smiled. "Anton will see you now." He stepped back from the open doorway, but before Dani could enter, Anton called out.

"Carter."

The attorney moved past her to stand in the doorway, and Dani saw a muscle flinch in his jaw.

"Check on Jim and see what kind of trouble he's in this time."

Carter nodded and stepped back, motioning for Dani to go in. She swallowed hard, mentally zipping over every facet of her "background," and certain she knew exactly what the long-ago sacrificial Christians had felt like when being ushered into the Roman arena toward the waiting lions.

The room was dimly lit, and Dani was forced to blink several times to accustom herself to the lack of light. She paused just inside of the room, and the door closed behind her, but she was barely aware of the soft click of the knob. Her gaze had been instantly drawn to an oil painting on the wall directly opposite where she stood. A soft light shone down from above it to illuminate the life-size portrait, causing it to become the focal point of the entire room. She found she had no need to read the tiny brass plaque attached to its frame to identify the four people the artist had caught with such perfection that they seemed nearly alive. Her gaze flitted over the older man and woman, who were, of course, the elder Reichards, and she had seen enough pictures in the society columns to know the young woman beside them was Anton's late sister, Sherry.

But it was the man who stood behind them, whose dark, French Creole looks had mesmerized her three years ago when she'd first read of the tragedy that had struck his family, who Dani found her gaze riveted upon now.

The artist had perfectly captured the air of insolent virility that had surrounded Anton Reichard in every picture Dani had ever seen of him. But what held her gaze was not the handsome features, jet-black hair, or broad shoulders. It was Anton's eyes she felt drawn to, and the glimmer within their smoky blue depths that hinted at an intense passion for life and love.

Memory of her dream invaded Dani's mind and brought a flush of warmth to her cheeks.

"Miss Lane."

The deep voice came from her right. Dani stiffened and turned, braced to confront him, yet not knowing quite what she expected . . . the seductive lover from her dream . . . the handsome man from the photos in the newspapers . . . the virile man in the portrait whose eyes hinted of endless passion . . . or the mysterious recluse who had cloistered himself away from the world and created a reputation for being ill-tempered and cold.

He stood several feet away, before a wall that was floor-to-ceiling shelves lined with leather-bound books. Half of his face was touched by the soft glow of a lamp on a nearby table, the other half steeped in shadow—shades of blue and gray that intensified each curve and line, and gave his features a hardness that was almost barbarous.

She knew instantly that he was none of the men she had feared him to be, and at the same time, he was all of them. Tall, dark, and patrician. The effect of his presence was like a charge of electricity dancing across her flesh, seizing her heart, and robbing her of breath. Power, raw and potent, seemed to surround him like a tangible aura, threatening to reach out and draw her into its sphere. And it wasn't a place she was at all certain she wanted to be.

A shudder coiled itself around Dani's spine, then splintered into a thousand shivers that shot through her entire body, head to toe, leaving her scalp tight, her hands trembling, and her legs feeling weak.

This was no portrait in oil, no image from a newspaper photo, and she found now that neither had prepared her for this man of flesh and blood. Those images had been of a man who'd lived in sunlight . . . but she sensed instantly that was not the man who stood only a few feet from her now.

Her gaze met his, and Dani found him staring at her. His blue-gray eyes were surrounded by an aureole of black, and looking into them, Dani couldn't help but think of the fog that, on a frigid winter's night, sometimes swept over the streets of San Francisco, where she'd gone to school. It could chill a person to the bone in seconds, and she had the distinct impression that Anton Reichard's eyes could do the same.

His brow was wide, his nose aquiline, giving him an air of aristocracy, but not quite enough to annul the rugged masculinity behind the facade of wealthy refinement. Dani sensed the coiled power in his tall frame, and in spite of telling herself not to, she ran her gaze over him head to toe. Black slacks accentuated long, lean legs, while a white silk shirt left little wonder as to the muscular contours of his physique.

Suddenly realizing she had been staring, Dani cleared her throat. "Mr. Reichard." She held out her hand as she walked toward him. "It's a pleasure to meet you."

Instead of a polite retort, his eyes darkened, and the coolness in them threatened to erupt into a turbulent storm from which she knew, instinctively, she would have no escape. She paused, unsure, then hurriedly admonished herself. She had the feeling she was moving toward the devil himself, but if that's what it was going to take to get this story, then so be it.

Anton ignored her offered hand and motioned for her to sit on one of the twin blue settees before him. At the movement, a lock of black hair fell onto his forehead. Dani stopped in midstride, once again assailed by the memory of her dream. A scathing heat surged through her. The collar of her silk blouse sliced into her throat and threatened to cut off her air. The garment's delicate threads suddenly felt as if they had become a solid cloak that was attempting to suffocate her. She could almost feel Anton Reichard's hands traveling the length of her body, igniting flames wherever they touched and leaving her breathless, anxious, writhing beneath his caresses and begging for more.

Her cheeks stung with the heat of a blush.

As if he sensed what she was thinking and feeling, one black brow migrated upward derisively, and the corners of his lips curled slightly.

It was then she noticed the thin scar that pierced through the left side of his upper lip, a minute line of jagged scar tissue that further heightened the look of enmity that emanated from him.

"My attorney thinks quite highly of your qualifications, Miss Lane. I must admit, however, that I have some reservations."

She saw a glimmer of satisfaction light his eyes as she started at his words.

"My reservations are not about your qualifications, Miss Lane, those are excellent. They are about you."

He let his last word hang in the air, a challenge waiting for her response.

Dani was instantly seized by the certainty that he knew everything, exactly who she was and why she had lied her way into his home. Most men she'd known would, in this situation, just say so if they knew of her deceit, then order her from their home. But Anton Reichard wasn't like most men she'd known. She had determined that long ago, the first time she'd seen his picture. Then his life had been an open book, now it was closed tight. He was an enigma, both to the world and to her.

So, if he did know who she really was, he was playing some sort of perverse cat-and-mouse game with her, following his rules and allowing Dani the time to strangle herself. She stiffened and threw up her chin. Well, *that* wasn't going to happen. "I can assure you, Mr. Reichard, you need have no reservations about me."

"Really? We've had a number of applicants apply for this position, Miss Lane, but quite frankly, several have seemed more interested in me than in the job."

Her knees felt as if they were going to buckle. She knew he was referring to a personal interest and hers was strictly a professional one—nevertheless, his point was too close to the truth for comfort. "I . . . That is not the case with me, Mr. Reichard. I can assure you that I'm interested only in a position of employment. Nothing more." A twinge of guilt cuffed her conscience, and she shrugged it away. Now was no time to develop idealistic scruples.

He approached her slowly, each step reinforcing her impression that this man was more graceful and fluid in motion than any she had ever seen—and much darker in spirit.

Dani swallowed hard and settled onto the settee, afraid if she didn't sit, her now trembling legs might give out beneath her. He paused only inches from where she sat, and Dani felt the heat of his body reach out and touch her. Butterfly wings suddenly erupted in her stomach, and her heartbeat lurched erratically before the organ seemed to flutter up and into her throat.

"Are you sure, *chère*, that the job is the only reason

you have come here?" He stared down at her, his gaze unflinching, demanding that she meet it, answer it, acquiesce to it. "That is the only reason?"

Dani was fully aware of the familiar endearment he'd used, but too preoccupied with trying to remain calm, at least outwardly, to worry about it.

To her surprise he suddenly reached out and touched the hand she had laid on the arm of the settee, slowly running his index finger along the thin bone that extended from her wrist to the tip of her middle finger.

Dani sucked in a sharp stab of breath as her skin felt as if his touch had set it afire. She dragged her hand away from his, clasping it about the other and shoving both into her lap, out of his reach, out of danger.

"Why would you want to seclude yourself out here, *chère?*" His tone had dropped to a seductive, deep purr that slid over her body, over her senses, like a taunting stroke of warm, luxuriant silk, smooth and enticing. "You're a beautiful woman, even though"—his gaze swept over her in blatant assessment—"you try hard to hide the fact. Even so, why would you want to be away from everything and everyone?"

She watched the cold smile return, the thin scar arcing jaggedly to emphasize the sardonic twist of his lips. "Or is it, Miss Lane, that like the other applicants we've interviewed, rather than being in search of a job, you are actually seeking a rich husband?"

Anger and indignation flared in Dani, battling for control of her better senses against the sudden and repeated flashes of the dream whose memory, along with his nearness, threatened to turn her own body traitorous with desire.

What was it about this man that unnerved her to the

point of distraction? She glared up at him. It had been foolish to believe she could match wits with the obvious mental prowess and cunning that a man like Anton Reichard possessed. He'd probably known exactly who she was since her initial interview with Carter Tyrene. Maybe even before, when they'd read the résumé she had sent in, carefully sprinkled with lies and omissions.

She tried to appear incensed. "Mr. Reichard, if you've already made up your mind not to hire me, then—"

"I haven't," he drawled easily. "But I would like an answer to my question."

Dani found his eyes threatening to pull her inside of them, to drown her within their brackish mists and leave her senses routed. "All right. I have no desire to be around people anymore, particularly friends and relatives," she said, forcing the words past suddenly dry lips.

A frown drew the wide expanse of golden skin and dark brows above his eyes downward, intensifying a look of malevolence that seemed to lurk behind every movement of his features. His gaze swooped to invade hers, as if trying to pierce through the flesh and bone that made up Dani "Lane" and see straight into her soul.

He wanted to uncover her secrets, and she wanted desperately to hug them to her and hide them from his prying senses.

"No desire to be around people," Anton said, repeating her words. He moved around the room, touching a table here, a book there, the back of a chair, the sash of a window. Each time he slowly, almost sensually, drew his finger across an object, Dani was reminded of how he had touched her hand in much the same way, and a warm, delicious shiver raced through her. At the window

he turned and walked toward his desk, an effortless suc-
cession of motion that Dani instantly found analogous to
a black panther she'd once seen upon a visit to the New
Orleans zoo. The creature had impressed her as incredi-
bly beautiful, but more than that, he'd been all strength,
grace, and dark danger . . . and that was the impression she had of Anton Reichard now as she watched him
move about the room.

The correlation brought forth a familiar sense of
dread.

His eyes remained downcast. Ebony lashes created
blue-black shadows upon subtly curved cheekbones,
adding to the illusion of darkness. At the corner of his
desk he paused. And while Dani couldn't be certain, she
thought he looked at her, though she saw neither his
eyes move, nor his lashes raise.

Suddenly she was assailed by the overwhelming sensation that she was being stalked, both mentally and
physically. He was a predator, like the cat she had compared him to, and if what her father was always saying
about her was true, that she wasn't strong enough to
handle real adversity, especially the kind thrust onto investigative journalists, then Anton Reichard would definitely devour her.

Dani's hands began to tremble, and she clasped them
together as the silence, and her uneasiness, dragged out
between them.

"Why?"

His demanding one-word question startled her, especially since she suddenly couldn't put it into perspective
and remember what they'd been discussing. "Why?" she
echoed dumbly. Why what? her mind screamed. Why
did she want this story? Why had she lied?

"Why don't you want to be around other people, Miss Lane? *Especially friends and relatives?*"

"Oh." She dropped her voice to inflect it with a tone of sadness. "I recently lost my husband and child, Mr. Reichard, and I find it difficult now to be around other people, especially those I've been close to. They don't know what to say . . . except that they're sorry." She looked up at him then, hoping her face had the right amount of despondency on it to be believable. "And that doesn't really help."

She saw the slight twitch of his brow, the flash of understanding that swept through his steely eyes like a bolt of lightning. It was there for only the briefest of milliseconds, but definitely there, and Dani knew she'd scored a point.

"Yes, Mr. Tyrene explained your background to me." He turned to stare at the bookshelves, his back to her.

Had she gone too far? An unexpected comber of guilt settled on her shoulders like a pair of massive hands, heavy and hard, weighing down on her conscience. Stan had been right, the bit about the husband and child had been too melodramatic, too cruel. But it was too late to call the lie back, even though she suddenly wished she could.

As abruptly as he'd turned away, Anton wheeled around to face her. "I'll need you to start right away, Miss Lane. Tonight. Would that be agreeable?"

"Tonight?" The dream flashed through Dani's mind.

"Yes. If you're to start first thing in the morning, it would be better if you moved your things to the plantation tonight. I start my day at six every morning and work here in my study. You'll have an office next door."

He motioned toward a door set into the far wall. "I stop at eleven and ride for an hour. Sanitee has lunch ready by noon, and I'm back here in my study by one."

She nodded. A strict routine. That could make things more difficult. The housekeeper would know when someone should be in the offices and when they shouldn't. Searching his files would not be easy under those circumstances.

"We'll finish up every day at four o'clock," he continued. "From that point on you will not try to contact or find me for any reason whatsoever, is that clear?" His eyes practically bored into hers.

"But what if there's an emer—"

"I said not for any reason, Miss Lane. If you cannot commit to that, then perhaps you are the wrong person for this position after all."

Dani inhaled deeply, trying to calm her suddenly panic-stricken senses. She was too close; she would not lose this story now because some absurd dream made her nervous. "No, no, that's fine, Mr. Reichard, really. After four you're"—she shrugged—"unreachable."

"Good. I usually return to the house by seven-thirty. Sanitee serves dinner at eight."

Dani nodded, but her curiosity was piqued. She'd always hated secrets. Even as a child, whenever one of her three brothers had had a secret she'd prodded, poked, pried, and driven all of them nuts until she found out what the secret was. And she hadn't been much better about keeping secrets either. To Dani, what good was knowing something if she couldn't tell it to someone else?

"Carter will drive you back to town now so you can

get your things," Anton said. "Sanitee will have your room ready when you return."

Dani rose.

He started to turn away, then paused and looked back at her. "I'm sorry for your loss, Miss Lane."

Her loss? For a split second Dani's mind remained completely blank, then she remembered her lie about losing a husband and a child and forced a solemn expression to her face. "Thank you, Mr. Reichard, I appreciate that."

A dark shadow swept over his features at her hesitation, and remained there as he watched her walk from the room. Instinct and the keen sense of wariness he'd developed over the past three years told him there was more to Danielle Lane than met the eye. Much more. But none of Carter's investigations had turned up anything overtly suspicious, and Carter was usually very thorough.

Nevertheless, there was something about her that wasn't right. Anton knew that. He had a feeling for such things. And he was rarely wrong. Turning back to his desk, he stared down at the phone. There was one person who might know something about Danielle Lane, might be able to answer some of his still-lingering questions about her, but he wondered if he dared make the call. After a few seconds' hesitation he shrugged mentally, and picked up the phone, quickly dialing a number he thought he'd never use again.

The phone rang several times. He was just about to conclude that she wasn't in and hang up, when she answered.

"Jessica, this is An . . . Tony." The sound of his old nickname felt strange on his tongue. Almost no one called him that anymore, but that had been his choice. He was no longer that person.

There was a long silence on the other end of the phone, and when she finally did respond her tone was cool, but at least she didn't hang up.

THREE

"I'm in, Stan!"

"Doesn't surprise me," he grumbled. "You're stubborn and determined, just like your old man. That's one of the reasons I hired you."

She knew the remark had been meant as a compliment, but Dani cringed nevertheless. Harlen Coroneaux was one of the best investigative journalists in the country. He was also her father, but she wasn't sure he'd ever really noticed that fact. He was always too busy with his job or her brothers.

Careerwise she was following in his footsteps, but he hadn't seemed to notice that either, and sometimes she wondered if she had gone into journalism because she loved it, or because she was trying to get her father's attention. She prayed it was the former, since the latter would most likely never happen.

Dani shook off the thought. "Listen, Stan, Reichard wants me back at his place tonight, so I'm packing, but two things first: One, do a check on Jim Knight, the man Sherry Reichard was engaged to marry. I think he's involved in this casino venture thing, and he's not very happy about it."

"Yeah, and?"

"And my car. I forgot about it, but what if Tyrene or Reichard checks with the DMV on my plates?"

"Tell them Coroneaux was your married name and hold your breath."

A picture of Anton Reichard flitted through her mind, and Dani felt certain that holding her breath wouldn't do any good if he got even a hint of the fact that she wasn't who and what she'd claimed to be.

She finished packing and, after a chat with her landlady, who agreed to water her plants until she returned, Dani drove away from her St. Charles Street apartment, a feeling of combined dread and excitement coursing through her.

It was a little past seven when she pulled her black Mustang up in front of Bayou Noir. The house was dark except for a pale glow of light filtering through the fanlight and two narrow windows that framed the entry door.

Uneasiness swept over her, and she absently rubbed her right hand over her forearm, finding her flesh covered with goose bumps. With the advent of darkness the place had taken on a sense of the macabre, and the eerie silence surrounding it only intensified the illusion.

"Great," Dani mumbled under her breath. "With the way my luck runs he's probably already found out who I am and they've all gone out to dinner." She opened the trunk. "Or, better yet, Reichard's just now climbing out of his coffin while Sanitee the voodoo queen is holding some kind of ritualistic ceremony in the attic, maybe sticking pins into a little doll who looks exactly like me."

She stared at her luggage and wished someone were around to help her with it, shrugged resolutely, and grabbed one of the suitcases.

Suddenly a loud scream, like that of a terrified child, rent the air. Dani jumped, lost her grip on the suitcase, and whirled around, straining to see past the shadows beneath the huge trees that dotted the landscape. Her heart had lodged solidly in her throat, though it was still pumping furiously and threatening to cut off her air and send her into a dead faint.

The scream came again.

Dani spun to dash for the house and nearly barreled into Sanitee.

"Welcome back, Miss Lane," the housekeeper said softly. Behind her a peacock strutted haughtily across the lawn, stopped, and with tail feathers fully plumed on magnificent display, screamed again.

Dani sat across the table from Anton and tried to think of something to say. She'd never been good at small talk, and he didn't seem to be making much of an effort, which left an uncomfortable silence hanging between them.

She chanced a look at him and found herself staring into the most emotionless pair of blue eyes she'd ever seen.

"I'm sorry the peacock frightened you, Miss Lane," Anton said, as he held her gaze. "We should have warned you about them, but then, I'd expected you back before dark."

Dani felt as if she'd been reprimanded. She opened her mouth, thought better of the sharp retort she'd been about to mutter, and reached for her wineglass instead. It wouldn't exactly be smart to give him reason to fire her. Then she'd lose the story.

He rose and tossed his napkin onto the table. "Well, if you'll excuse me, Miss Lane, I have a few things I need to see to before . . ."

"Meow."

They both turned toward the doorway to the foyer to see a large, sleek black cat saunter into the room. The animal's short hair, like planes of ebony satin, reflected the chandelier's light in a sweep of shimmering curves, while the tip of its long tail flicked at the air. Approaching to within a few feet of the table, the cat paused and stared up at Dani, its vibrant green eyes seeming to meet and lock with her own.

Dani shifted uncomfortably in her chair, hoping the animal, who she realized now was the size of a small dog and had to weigh at least twenty pounds, came no closer.

With an air of haughty indifference the cat blinked lazily and turned its attention to Anton.

"*Pichouette*," Anton said. "*Viens ici.*" He bent down, his extended hand emphasizing the spoken invitation for the animal to "come here."

Dani noticed that for the very first time since she'd met him, Anton's deep drawl actually had a caress of warmth to it. The sensation touched her in a way it shouldn't have, in a way she didn't want it to. She watched him bend and scoop the cat up and into his arms, and Dani's fingers twisted nervously about in her lap.

"Little Girl," she said, translating the feline's Creole name into English. "Strange name for such a large cat."

Anton held the animal cradled in one arm while his free hand lovingly stroked the back of her head, then slid down so that his fingers could caress the animal's throat as it stretched its neck out in offering.

A loud purr broke the silence as Pichouette closed her eyes and leaned into Anton's touch. He smiled, and the transformation that came over his face was suddenly fascinating and, surprisingly, a bit heartrending.

"She was the runt of the litter," he said.

Too bad she didn't stay that way, Dani thought, and shuddered as the cat's eyes suddenly opened and stared at her as if it had heard her thoughts.

Anton looked back at Dani, and she had the uneasy feeling that he had heard her thoughts too. His gaze moved over her, like the molding of liquid steel to her flesh, hot and burning, filling every pore, every cell and fiber of her being. But she knew, intuitively, that the look wasn't meant to seduce her. He was not only look-ing *at* her, but *inside* her, and the realization was un-nerving.

Dani felt a chill move through her body like wintry water rippling over a shallow streambed. She didn't want to be at Bayou Noir Plantation, alone with a man who had sequestered himself away from the world, who lived within dark thoughts and even darker emotions. The story wasn't that important. There were other stories. Safer stories. The thought surprised her, but not as much as the charge of emotions that seemed to have sprung up between her and the man standing only a few feet from her.

She rose quickly, nearly knocking over her wineglass and forgetting the napkin that had draped her lap. The square of intricately embroidered Italian cloth fluttered to the floor. "I really am tired, Mr. Reichard, so . . ." She glanced at the cat again and found it still staring at her. Dani's stomach flip-flopped, and her trembling hands curled into tight fists at her sides as she made for the doorway. "If you'll excuse me, I'll say good night."

"Miss Lane."

She paused and looked back at him, hoping he couldn't see the sudden panic she'd been unable to suppress.

"I didn't mean to make you nervous."

She forced a smile to her lips. "It's just first-day-on-the-job jitters, that's all," Dani said. "I'll be fine in the morning."

He took a step toward her. "If there's anything you need . . ." The cat jumped from his arms to the floor, and Dani shrieked, stepping back hurriedly as the animal dashed past her on its way toward the foyer.

She looked back at Anton and found him frowning. "Sorry, it . . . startled me."

"Are you certain it was the cat who frightened you, Miss Lane"—he smiled as his steely eyes burned into hers—"and not me?" His voice was so deep and rich and low that Dani not only heard it, but felt it glide seductively over her skin.

She shivered and turned back toward the doorway.

Dani stared at herself in the bathroom mirror. "You are not afraid of cats." The words sounded great, even convincing; unfortunately, she knew that's all they were:

Words. Her hands were still trembling, and her heart had yet to resume a normal beat. Though she knew all too well that those things couldn't be totally attributed to a reaction to the cat. She was attracted to Anton Reichard. It was crazy, it was ridiculous, but she couldn't deny that it was true.

She looked back at her image in the mirror. "Fine, so don't deny it. Ignore it, and get on with what you came here to do." She narrowed her eyes and glared at herself. "But why does he have to have a blasted cat?"

Memory of the animal made her shudder. They were hunters. Single-minded predators who stalked their quarry relentlessly, struck swiftly, and killed. They couldn't be trusted. None of them. Ever.

When she'd been five she hadn't thought that way. She'd had a cat. Ralph had been a big longhaired, lovable orange tom, and Dani's best friend. Until he ate Fred, her little white mouse, and second best friend. Dani had caught Ralph in the act, screamed, and swatted at him to make him stop.

Practically startled out of one of his nine lives, Ralph had whirled, hair standing on end, screeched loudly, and swatted back, scraping a huge paw, nails extended, across Dani's temple. Her resulting scream and her mother's swinging broom had sent Ralph flying through the kitchen's cat-door, and he hadn't come back for days. But it would have been fine with Dani if he hadn't come back at all.

Her temple had required a visit to the doctor, medicine that had stung so badly, she'd cried for hours, shots and stitches that had made her cry even harder, and another shot that had left her arm bruised and sore. The episode had left her with not only a dislike of cats, but a fear of them that was so intense, she was usually on the verge of panic even at seeing one in the distance.

"You are not afraid of cats, and you are not attracted to Anton Reichard," she said to herself again, and wished she could believe her own words. A long sigh escaped her lips. "And the moon is made of green cheese." She moved into the spacious bedroom Sanitee had shown her to earlier and lay down on the poster bed that nearly dominated the room, slipping her legs beneath a lace-trimmed coverlet.

After almost an hour of staring up at the pink silk canopy overhead and finding sleep elusive, Dani threw back the covers and rose. The room was too stuffy and dim. She turned the knob on the bedside lamp to its next notch and the bulb in the etched pink glass shade brightened, its light invading and conquering the shadows that had hovered about the room's corners and antique furnishings.

Moving to the French doors that led to the second floor gallery, Dani threw them open and walked outside. The warm night air touched her skin gently and wafted through the long tendrils of her dark hair like the caressing fingers of an impassioned lover. She stood at the gallery's rail, resting her hands lightly on its smooth white surface. A yawn swelled within her chest, and she stretched wide to release it, lifting her arms as if reaching for the sky, and letting her head drop back upon her shoulders. Her breasts thrust forward, and the taut peak of each pushed against the sheer blue silk of her nightgown. As the yawn slipped from her lips in a soft whoosh, Dani sighed contentedly and stared dreamily up at what appeared to be a thousand bright stars sprinkled across the stygian blackness of the night sky.

Standing within the shadows beneath one of the moss-draped oaks that grew at the edge of the lawn surrounding the mansion, Anton stared up at Dani. He had been on his way back to the house from a walk and had stopped upon seeing her on the gallery. Watching her now, he felt something stir inside of him.

A small voice in the back of his mind whispered a warning, cautioning him to look away, but he paid it no heed. His body was hot and hard with desire, and that was a feeling he had sworn never to allow himself to experience again—or at least not give in to. He would not love another woman, emotionally or physically. That was his self-imposed penance. He would go through the rest of his life alone. It was the only way he could even hope to live with what he'd done.

He was about to step away from the tree, to move farther into the shadows of the gardens beyond and out of sight of her when he noticed that Dani seemed to be staring down at him. She couldn't actually see him, he knew that, yet he couldn't shake the feeling that her gaze had locked with his. He felt the breath catch in his throat as his body throbbed with an instant and fiery need. He should never have let Carter talk him into hiring her.

His gaze drifted over the curvaceous lines of her body, outlined against the sheer nightgown by the pale light emanating from the open French doors behind her. A surge of passion assailed him, filled him, and momentarily overshadowed every dark thought and thread of common sense that he possessed.

Staring at her now, Anton imagined his hands gliding over the rounded swell of her breasts, his thumbs flicking taunting touches upon rosy nipples that seemed to be straining against her gown and beckoning to him. He could almost feel his legs entwined about hers, the hot sheen of her naked body pressed to his, the hard, throbbing lust that was his pushing into her, filling her, melding them together.

Suddenly a blaring wail split the night air.

Dani, startled, whirled about in search of what had made the almost unearthly noise. It was obvious that she knew what it sounded like, but it was also obvious that she reasoned her conclusion impossible. She ran to the end of the gallery, looking out at the gardens.

Anton watched as the sheer silk of her gown billowed out around her, furling about her long legs, the delicate curve of each fold catching the moonlight and reflecting it in shimmering cascades of light that made her, momentarily, appear a diaphanous illusion.

With the return of the night's silence, which seemed now almost so extreme as to be eerie, Dani ran back across the gallery toward the open French doors and hurriedly disappeared inside.

Glancing over his shoulder toward the inky depths of the bayou, Anton smiled to himself. He had tried numerous times over the past few months to dissuade Sheba from doing that, especially at night, but she was young and stubborn, and it was her way of calling to him.

Looking back at the now empty gallery, he found

himself suddenly overcome by a more intense sense of loneliness than he had felt in a very long time.

The acknowledgment of it made him angry. He needed peace, quiet, and solitude, not the kind of torment having Dani Lane around every day would subject him to. "Damn you, Carter," he snarled quietly. "Damn you."

Dani sat huddled on the huge bed with her legs drawn up, arms wrapped around them, chin resting on her knees. Someone had been watching her while she'd stood on the gallery. She hadn't felt their gaze on her until only seconds before she'd run back into the bedroom, but that had been long enough for her to be certain.

Restless, she glanced at the small travel clock she'd set on the nightstand. It was nearing midnight, yet she was no closer to sleep than she had been three hours earlier when she'd retreated to the elegantly appointed room. She sat on the bed, listening to the house for almost a half an hour. No sound interrupted the silence, which she hoped meant that Sanitee and Anton Reichard had retired for the night.

Kicking aside the blanket that covered her feet, she slipped from the bed and tiptoed back to the French doors. But this time she didn't go out, or even stand directly in front of the window. Instead she remained behind one of the heavy drapes and peeked around it at the moonswept gardens. Her gaze roamed the scene at length, slowly, pausing upon every shadow, but she had no sense now that anyone was looking back at her. And there had been no repeat of that sound she knew couldn't possibly have been what it sounded like.

Her gaze continued to move over the shadow-dappled landscape, appreciating the beauty of the various foliage and the way the moonlight reflected silver as it touched the large dark and waxy leaves of the magnolia trees, shimmered like gold upon the smaller point-edged leaves of the oaks, and sprinkled itself like stardust across a portion of the emerald-green lawn.

Dani looked toward the area where she thought she'd seen someone standing earlier. Shadows swayed everywhere as a soft breeze riffled through the long curtains of Spanish moss that draped almost every tree branch in sight. But she could discern no human silhouette, feel no dark eyes staring at her from the blackness.

Most likely she'd let her imagination get the better of her. She was about to turn away from the window and go downstairs, intent on searching Reichard's study, when a movement in the gardens caught her eye. It was so fleeting, she wasn't certain she'd really even seen it, until the woman, whose flowing black gown melded with the night to make her nearly indistinguishable from the dark, skipped through a sliver of moonlight that played upon the gown's threads and turned them momentarily translucent. Dani watched as she neared the edge of the lawn and a man suddenly stepped into view from beneath one of the trees. He drew her into his embrace. A second later the couple disappeared into the shadows.

Dani moved away from the window. As far as she knew, Sanitee was the only other woman at Bayou Noir, so that must have been her. But who was the man, and if he was her lover, why was it necessary for her to meet him in the dead of night? Dani shrugged. It wasn't any of her business, and she had other things to think about, such as did she dare go down to Anton's study now? His schedule made it nearly impossible to get into the office and his files any other time without taking the risk of being discovered by the housekeeper.

Dani frowned, trying to decide what to do, then opened her overnight bag and retrieved the small pinpoint flashlight she'd brought with her. Sanitee could be out all night, and Dani didn't have time to waste trying to make up her mind and get up her courage. She slipped from her room and hurried down the hall.

The house was dark, the foyer stairs illuminated only by the faint moonlight that shone through the entry's fanlight window. She said a prayer of thanks to find the door to Reichard's study unlocked, but upon entering the room, couldn't decide where to start her search. She glanced at his desk, the bookshelves that lined the wall, then at the oak file cabinets set against another wall. Dani nodded to herself. That's where she needed to start. She took the flashlight from her pocket and flicked it on, then opened the first drawer of the cabinet and shone the light onto the files.

There were dozens, all alphabetized. She wanted the file pertaining to Reichard's casino venture. This drawer ended before "C." She quietly slid the drawer closed and opened the next. The file was one of the first in the drawer. Dani breathed a sigh of relief that it hadn't been filed under some corporate name she didn't know. She held the flashlight between her lips and pulled the thick and somewhat unwieldy folder from the drawer with both hands, laid it atop the others, and began to riffle through it. The first thing she saw was a partnership agreement.

"Having trouble sleeping, Miss Lane?"

Dani's heart nearly stopped as she whirled around, her gaze darting about the shadows in search of him in the dark. When he reached to turn on the lamp that sat on the table next to him, she finally saw him sitting in one of the tall wing chairs by the fireplace.

FOUR

She hadn't slept a wink. He should have fired her when he caught her riffling through his files in the dead of night, and he hadn't, which had her worried. Dani had stammered out an excuse of not being able to sleep and figuring she'd get a jump on being organized for her new job by acquainting herself with the organization of his files. It had been a lame excuse at best. He hadn't said he didn't believe her, but she had seen the skepticism in his eyes. All he'd said, however, was that she would have plenty of opportunity and time to familiarize herself with his office in the morning. Then he'd merely stared at her until she nodded, said good night, and left his study.

Now it was morning and time to face him again. She wasn't looking forward to that. Dani checked herself in the mirror one more time before leaving her room. She'd chosen to wear a femininely cut silk blouse of deep blue with matching slacks, knowing the color intensified that of her eyes, for all the good that would do her if he ordered her to pack up and leave. She walked to the door, then changed her mind and retraced her steps. Taking her cellular phone from her overnight bag, she dialed Stan's private number.

He answered on the second ring.

"Stan, Dani. Did you find out anything on Jim Knight?"

"He's one of Reichard's partners in the casino investment."

"I suspected that. What else?"

"Looks like his personal financial status is pretty rocky. If Reichard pulls out of that deal now, Knight goes right down the tubes."

"But what about his family's money? Aren't the Knights one of the wealthiest families in Texas?"

"Yeah, but I said his *personal* financial status. The way I hear it, the old man refuses to bail Jim out of any more bad deals. Seems that ever since his fiancée died . . ."

"Sherry Reichard," Dani said.

"Yeah, ever since she died, he's put his money into one bad investment after another."

"Stan, I need you to check something else out. Last night I saw Reichard's housekeeper sneak out of the house and meet someone."

"Who?"

"I couldn't see him. But I'd like to know who it was."

"What's your line?"

"Well, it could be nothing more than she can't get away from the house so her lover comes to her. Or it could be that she's seeing someone she figures her employer wouldn't approve of her seeing, like one of his competitors."

"Or it could be," Stan offered, "that she's making a little money on the side selling off info on Reichard."

"Or being used," Dani countered. She thought about her conversation with Stan as she walked down the wide staircase of Bayou Noir and let the tempting smell of bacon and eggs lead her into the dining room. She wasn't looking forward to sitting at the table and trying to make small talk with Reichard again, but as she entered the long room she realized that wasn't going to be a problem, because it was empty.

Anton watched Dani as she opened the same file drawer he'd watched her go through the previous night and retrieved the folder he'd requested. His gaze moved over the tantalizing shape her back presented to him. She was not tall, he guessed her at five four, but her legs were the kind that a man dreamed of wrapping his own around, and her hips were curved just enough to tease a man's senses.

The heat of want curled about his loins, and Anton shifted uncomfortably on his chair. Passion might be the uppermost concern of his body, but suspicion was the uppermost thing on his mind. She had only been at Bayou Noir for a matter of hours, but it was long enough for him to know that he was in trouble, in more ways than one. His instinct at the moment was the same as it had been the night before when he'd watched her riffling through his files. He'd wanted to fire her then, and he wanted to fire her now, but he held back, because if he did that, he might never know who'd sent her to spy on him, and he was sure that's exactly what she was doing.

He had no doubt that everything she'd told Carter was a lie, but being certain of that didn't tell him who she was, who she was working for, or what she was hoping to discover.

That wasn't the only reason he wasn't sending her packing, however, and he was smart enough not to try to convince himself it was. He didn't want to want her, but he couldn't deny he did. His desire stirred up feelings in him that he'd sworn to leave behind, dead and buried with the life he no longer had, with the family he'd killed. A knot of emotion caught in Anton's throat.

Dani Lane, or whoever she was, reminded him of a past he didn't want to remember, of a woman who had stirred him to such recklessness, it had plunged his life into a dark swell of disaster. He had betrayed his own family because of his desire for a woman and—

"Here's the file you wanted," Dani said, cutting into Anton's thoughts. She held a folder out to him.

He took it and set it down on his desk as the phone near his hand rang.

Dani automatically reached for it, but Anton's hand curled around the receiver first. "It's my private line."

Dani nodded and moved several feet from the desk but didn't leave the room.

"Yes?" Anton said into the phone. Only a few people had this number, and he had a pretty good idea which one was calling.

"It's Jessica."

"I've been waiting for your call, Jess," Anton said. "What did you find?"

Dani went cold at his words. She knew it was ridiculous to feel such paranoia, knew that he could be talking to anyone about anything. He could be about to discuss one of his business ventures, or something to do with one of his companies, but she couldn't help wondering if his conversation with "Jess" was really about Danielle "Lane" Coroneaux.

She clasped her hands together behind her back to keep him from seeing that they were trembling and wished desperately she could hear what the person on the other end of the line was saying.

"A lot, uh?" Anton said. He grabbed for pen and paper and motioned to Dani that she could leave the room. "Okay, start."

Dani walked slowly to the door, feeling the need now more than ever to listen to his conversation.

"Oh, I'll tell you everything in exactly three minutes," Jessica said. Her light laughter danced merrily through the phone line. "Which is how long it will take me to get to your place from where I am on the road."

A click followed, and Anton knew she'd hung up so that he couldn't tell her not to come. He looked up at Dani. "Jessica Beausoil is on her way. Please show her into my office when she arrives. You can take a break while she's here."

Surprised, Dani merely nodded and walked to the room that was her office. Jessica Beausoil. Dani knew the name. Anton had been seeing Jessica steadily for months before the accident. The society columnists had predicted they'd marry, but they hadn't. They'd remained together for a few months after the plane crash, but not for long. Anton had sequestered himself in Bayou Noir, and Jessica had begun a continuous round of dating almost every available bachelor in New Orleans.

So why was she coming to Bayou Noir now? Dani wondered. And even more puzzling, why was Anton seeing her when everything Dani had learned about him led her to believe he didn't see anyone other than Carter Tyrene and Floyd Pellichet?

Dani sat down behind her desk, then rose immediately when the door to her office opened and a tall blonde whose perfect features looked sculpted from porcelain walked in. "Oh, you must be the new secretary."

Dani held out her hand. "Yes, Dani Lane."

Jessica touched Dani's hand with the tips of fingers whose long nails were painted a brilliant red, then turned toward the door that led to Anton's office. Before opening it, she looked back at Dani. "Miss Lane, have Sanitee bring Anton and me some coffee, would you?"

The door closed, and Dani stared at it. She had taken an instant and thorough dislike to Jessica Beausoil, and she couldn't have explained why. What she did know was that the feeling left her wondering if Sanitee had any arsenic in the kitchen Dani could rub into Jessica's coffee cup.

"She didn't go to the University of Southwestern Louisiana, Tony."

Anton's eyes narrowed as he looked at the woman he'd once thought he couldn't live without. There was no passion left between them, at least none that he could feel, and he wondered at that. It had once been so strong, so overpowering. He forced the puzzle from his mind and turned his concentration to what she was saying. "You're sure about that, Jess?"

"Darling, you said she claims to have graduated USL the same year as me, but that's impossible because she's not in any of my yearbooks." Jessica crossed one long, lithe leg over the other. "Now I could understand her not being in one yearbook if she was busy the day the pictures were taken or something, but Tony, she isn't in any of them. And I even called a few friends to see if they remembered her from school, you know, just in case she transferred in late as a senior or something. No one remembered her."

"Still . . ."

"Oh, I knew you'd say that," Jessica said, flipping a hand in the air, "so I called the dean. He's a good friend of Daddy's and was more than willing to help. Anyway, there was never a Danielle Lane registered at USL—ever."

Anton stood. "I appreciate your doing this for me, Jess, really."

"Good, then you won't mind taking me to dinner at Brennan's tonight."

He shook his head. "I'm sorry, Jess, you know I can't do that."

Her china-blue eyes bored into his. "Can't or won't, Tony?" she challenged, standing to face him across the wide desk.

He saw the hurt behind the proud exterior she wore and knew he'd put it there, but it was too late to do anything about it. Nothing could change what had happened, and every time he looked at Jessica it was a reminder of what he'd done. He'd tried to shoulder all the blame himself for what had happened, but there was a part of him, a small part he couldn't control, that blamed her too. Anton sighed. "Does it really matter, Jess?"

"When you called I hoped . . ." She shrugged. A tear sparkled in the corner of one eye but didn't fall. "I guess I shouldn't have." She walked toward the door, paused before opening it, and looked back at him. "Don't call me anymore, Tony. Please."

♦ Dani watched Jessica Beausoil leave. She'd tried to hear their conversation through the closed door but had given up after being frustrated at catching nothing more than a few muffled words. Rising now, she walked back into Anton's office with the faint hope that he'd say something about why the woman he used to date had come calling.

"It's eleven," he said, his tone gruff. "Time to break." He strode toward the door to the foyer, yanked it open, then looked back at her. He knew what he was about to do was a mistake, but he wanted to know why Dani Lane was at Bayou Noir, and at whose instigation. "Come riding with me."

Dani didn't know whether it was an invitation or a command, but she nodded. Maybe, once they were out, relaxed and away from the house, he'd feel like talking. "I'll change and be down in a few minutes."

"I'll meet you at the stable."

Dani came around a curve in the path leading to the stable and paused. Just inside the open barn door, Anton was crouched beside a large black stallion. An older man hunkered beside him and held the horse's reins as Anton ran an assessing hand up and down one of the animal's rear legs. Dani saw instantly that Anton had changed clothes too. Sunlight shone on the back of the white sports shirt he wore, accentuating the pristine threads as well as the muscular contours they covered but failed to obscure.

Her steps sounded on the crushed oyster shells that covered the pathway between house and stable.

Anton rose and turned to her. The groom disappeared into the stable.

Dani smiled. "I hope I didn't keep you waiting."

His gaze pinned hers as he absently ran a hand through the loose tendrils of black hair that had fallen onto his forehead. He shouldn't have asked her to ride with him, but he knew with a certainty that angered him beyond normal reason, that even if he didn't suspect her of duplicity, he would have asked her to go with him this morning. "You do know how to ride?"

His tone made the question almost a snarling accusation.

She nodded. "It's been a while, but I used to do okay at it."

"Good. I've got Tom saddling Lady Jane for you." Anton turned back to the stallion and, lifting one stirrup and hooking it onto the saddle horn, began to tighten the cinch.

The groom appeared at the entrance of the stable then, and Dani looked at the horse he led toward her, a diminutive dapple gray mare with a beautiful black mane and tail. The animal nickered at Dani and shook her head, as if in invitation. "Lady Jane," Dani said, rubbing a hand over the horse's velvet-soft muzzle, "you really are a beauty, aren't you?"

The mare whinnied and pawed a foot on the ground.

"You may have to hold her on a tight rein for a while," Anton said. "She hasn't had a good ride since . . ."

Dani looked up as Anton's voice died away without his having finished the sentence. She saw the dark shadow that passed over his face, and darted a questioning look at the groom.

He leaned toward her, running a finger over his bushy gray mustache before saying in a hushed whisper, "Lady Jane was his sister's horse."

Dani nodded her understanding. She slipped her left foot into the stirrup and swung up and onto the saddle, thankful that it was western style. She had never been comfortable on those small English things. "So, where are we off to?" she asked lightly.

Anton mounted and looked down at her from his seat upon the large stallion. "I don't usually plan where I ride, Miss Lane, I just ride."

"Fine," she snapped a little too curtly, "you lead, and I'll follow." Unless you decide to ride into hell, she thought, remembering the darkness that came so easily and frequently to his features. Then she would definitely head in the opposite direction, story or no story.

They rode in silence for over half an hour, by which time Dani had no idea where she was. After a while everything looked the same, no matter which direction she looked. Trees, moss, snaking rivers of murky water, and still, dark shadows broken only by pallid beams of sunlight that occasionally pierced the thick growth of tree limbs overhead. Breaking suddenly into a clearing, Anton reined in, and Dani brought her horse to a stop beside his.

"It's beautiful," she said, looking around at the small open meadow.

He nodded in acknowledgment of her words but said nothing.

Dani watched him from the corner of her eye as he stared straight ahead, as if lost in thought, then turned abruptly, his eyes catching hers before she could look away.

"Why are you here?" he asked, his voice calm but threaded with steel.

A flash of alarm surged through Dani at the question. She tried to smile. "Be . . . because you asked me to ride with you," she said, pretending not to understand the true meaning of his words.

He dismounted and tossed his reins over a nearby bush. "We can rest here awhile before heading back." He walked around Lady Jane and stopped beside her.

Dani swung her right leg over the saddle and began to dismount. She felt his hands circle her waist and momentarily stilled. Emotion ran rampant through her at his touch; fear and excitement melding, heating her blood and burning her cheeks. Her left foot slipped in the stirrup, and she stumbled, falling against him. He caught her easily, holding her back pressed to the wide breadth of his chest.

For the passing of what seemed like an eternity, but was merely several very long seconds, Dani made no effort to move from his arms. She felt his heartbeat against her back, his hands, hot and burning on her rib cage, his breath stirring the wisps of hair at her temple that were too short to remain secured within the ribbon at her nape . . . and she wondered what it would be like to be kissed by him.

The thought brought reality crashing back upon her with a thud. Kissing Anton Reichard was the last thing in the world she wanted to do. Dani yanked her foot out of the stirrup and twisted in his arms in an effort to stand on her own two feet.

But he didn't release her. Not wanting to, but unable to resist, she looked up and found his lips all too near her own, his eyes looking down at her with that same intense glimmer she'd seen in his portrait. She felt his hands on her back pull her toward him. His hot breath played upon her cheek and the sensitive flesh of her lips, as if teasing them.

"Why are you here?" Anton said again, a haunting whisper she had no time to respond to as, like a hawk who swoops with lightning speed to claim its prey, Anton's lips captured hers. It was a kiss she was not prepared for, a kiss that was more demanding, more virile and fervent than any she'd ever known.

His probing tongue filled her mouth, and his arms deepened their embrace. She was crushed against his body so tightly that she could feel the racing beat of his heart, the raggedness of his breath, and the swell of desire that drove him.

Almost against her will Dani's hands slid up and over the well-honed contours of Anton's arms, not to push him away, but to pull him closer. Sanity and reason were suddenly no longer a part of her world, yet at the same time her senses were heightened to the point that she was aware of everything. The silence that surrounded them wasn't truly silent, but broken by the hum of creatures that made the bayou their home, the air that was already becoming heavy with the heat of the oncoming afternoon, and the heady, almost euphoric scents of the lush foliage that grew all around them.

But more than anything, she was aware of him—of the way his flesh felt against hers, the strength of his arms as they held her pressed to him, the soft, yet chafing caress of his lips, and the way he smelled of exotic spices and masculine power, an aroma she found both intoxicating and satisfying.

His mouth, his hands, his body were quickly becoming all that existed for her . . . and all she wanted.

A soft groan of pent-up need rumbled deep in Anton's throat. Why he had drawn her into his arms, why he had kissed her, he had no idea, but now that he had, the last thing he wanted to do was let her go. He had wanted this since the first moment he'd seen her, and now that he had claimed what he'd wanted, he took his time kissing her, savoring each line of softness within her lips, each curve of warmth and offering. Nothing else mattered but that this woman in his arms had, at least for the moment, driven the darkness from his soul.

Every male cell in his body was on fire with the need of her. Every good intention he'd had was burned away, vanquished the moment she'd opened her mouth to his, the moment her hands had seared their imprint upon his shoulders, holding him to her.

The rustling of a bush nearby was only a soft sound breaking the near total silence, but it was enough to drag Anton's senses back to reality. He stiffened and, wrapping his strong hands around Dani's arms, pulled away.

FIVE

Sanitee hurried away from the clearing and took the shortcut back to the house, her suspicions confirmed. Anton might not trust Danielle Lane, but he desired her, and that was nearly as dangerous. A curse, directed at Carter for bringing a woman like that to Bayou Noir, tumbled in a harsh whisper from Sanitee's lips. Danielle Lane was trouble, and Sanitee knew exactly what she was going to do about it.

"That was a mistake."

Dani stared at Anton as he spun away from her and strode toward his horse.

"I'm heading back to the house." He grabbed the stallion's reins and, when Dani didn't answer, turned to glance at her. At that moment the thin scar that marred the left side of his upper lip seemed to writhe to life, and his gaze, having caught hers in a merciless glower, darkened until the blue of his eyes was almost as black as any night she'd ever known.

"Unless you want to trust Lady Jane to lead you back, which she may or may not do, since she seems contented to remain here and graze, I suggest you get mounted." He smiled then, but it was barely a chill movement of his lips, imbued with no humor or warmth. For the very first time Dani saw and recognized the dark rage that burned beneath the surface of Anton's usually collected demeanor. But why kissing her had brought it on, she had no clue.

She hurried to her own horse, thankful to turn her back to Anton so that he couldn't see the flush of self-loathing she knew had come to her face as a result of his curt rebuff. Tears of humiliation stung her eyes, and she blinked quickly in an effort to hold them at bay. How could she ever have thought to kiss a man like Anton Reichard?

All of the articles she'd read about him, written before the tragedy, had described him as New Orleans's most devastatingly handsome, charming, and debonair bachelor. A ladies' man. Outgoing and happy. Except for the fact that he was still devastatingly handsome, that Anton Reichard obviously no longer existed. He had become a man who never smiled. He didn't bother with charm, he wasn't outgoing, and he definitely wasn't happy.

The moment she settled into her saddle Anton jerked the reins of his horse and spurred the animal into a loping gallop. Within seconds they had left the cheerful, sunlit clearing and plunged back into the bayou, instantly engulfed within its tenebrous shadows and eerily primitive spirit.

Beneath his breath Anton spat a series of curses. He'd brought her to the clearing in the hope that the serene atmosphere would relax her enough so that they could talk casually, and in doing so that she might say something that would give him a clue as to what she was up to, or who had sent her to Bayou Noir. Instead he'd lost all sense of reason and self-control and acted the fool.

The moment he'd held her in his arms and felt her body next to his, there had been only one thing on his mind. The mere thought of what he'd done sent his blood pressure soaring and ignited his temper with a self-condemning fury that was palpable. There was no room in his life for any more mistakes, yet he had just made a crucial and unforgivable one. But at least it hadn't been deadly, like the last.

He spurred his horse into a faster pace.

Dani Lane was a weakness Anton could not tolerate, yet he couldn't dismiss her without knowing the truth. There were too many questions he needed answered, and he knew that she just might be the key to the problems that had begun to surround him. Yet having her around was a temptation he now knew would take all of his willpower to resist.

In the past three years, because of his grief and the guilt that refused to give him any peace of mind, he had walked away from everything except his home and his business, and he hadn't really been paying enough attention to either of those. But he wasn't really interested in them. They were merely a necessity, a place to live and a means for providing him with what he needed to care for the others. *They* were what mattered.

Anton frowned at the thoughts milling through his mind. Ever since the accident he'd trusted only a handful of people to see to the things he didn't want to be bothered with, mainly Carter, Floyd, and Sanitee. Lately, however, as he'd begun to suspect that something was wrong and had started to take more interest in things, he had begun to realize what a mistake blind trust could be. Especially when he'd come to suspect that what was wrong might not be a case of a simple mistake, or of a competitor's taking advantage of his lack of interest in business, but that he'd been betrayed.

What he didn't know was by whom . . . Carter or Floyd? But was it possible that it was someone else? Jim, perhaps. He hadn't wanted to take Jim in as a partner in the casino venture because he knew Jim couldn't afford to lose, if it came to that. But he'd felt obligated, because he also knew his sister would have wanted him to give Jim the chance to make up for all the losses he'd suffered recently because of his deep grief over losing her. Sherry had meant everything to Jim, they'd been like soul mates, and Anton had taken her away from him. Allowing Jim to invest in the casino venture had been the least he could do. Now he wondered if that had been a mistake.

The only person he felt he could truly still trust was Sanitee. She had grown up on Bayou Noir and taken her place as the Reichards' head housekeeper when her mother had died five years earlier. She had nothing to do with his business. Yet there were things he wasn't willing to entrust even to her.

Dani stood beside the closed door of her office. The afternoon had passed in cold silence, except for a whirl of dictated letters about selling off this or that property, rents being due, a stock being sold, or Anton's occasional requests for files, ledgers, or notebooks. She wasn't certain exactly what he was doing or trying to do, but whatever it was, he was determined, and he hadn't taken a break at all until a moment ago when he'd asked her to leave him. Curious, she pressed her ear to the door, expecting to hear him talking on the phone. Instead she heard a short beep, followed by the buzz of the fax machine. *Then* she heard him on the phone.

"Dammit, numbers don't lie, Beau," Anton fairly snarled. "See what you can do. I need to know what this means, and I need to know pretty damned quick, or this could turn into the disaster Jim Knight already thinks it is."

Dani frowned. Who in the hell was Beau? And what was it Anton needed to know quickly?

He said something else, but it was too low for her to hear. Dani glanced at her own phone. The extension light that was usually lit when Anton was on-line had gone out, meaning he'd hung up. The door beside her suddenly opened, and Dani jumped back, hot with guilt as she looked up and saw in his eyes that he knew she'd been eavesdropping.

"I, uh, it's nearly four, so I was coming to see if you wanted anything else before I locked up."

"No. Yes. Call Carter and tell him I want to see him here this evening."

Dani made the call, telling Carter to come at eight-thirty. He didn't like it, grumbled about having to break a date, but he agreed, and Dani got the impression that he knew saying *no* was not an option. Hanging up, she headed upstairs to change into a pair of jeans. If she was going to follow Anton and find out where he went every day at four, she had to hurry.

By the time she got back downstairs the house was silent. She walked to the entry door, opened it, and looked outside, overcome by disappointment. "Damn, how could he have changed and gotten out of the house so fast?"

The moment the question slipped from her lips, she heard voices coming from the kitchen. Tiptoeing across the foyer, Dani stood against the wall beside the closed swinging door.

"Jack said she's doing fine."

Dani recognized Anton's voice instantly.

"But he's meeting me out there today to take another look at her, just in case she needs another shot against infection."

Dani gently pushed the door open a crack and peeked past the doorjamb.

"Here," Sanitee said, handing Anton a canvas sack, "I put some treats in there, and a thermos of boiling hot water, just in case Jack needs it for cleaning her wounds."

Dani watched as Anton hoisted the sack over one shoulder. "Thanks, Sanitee, they'll appreciate it. I'll see you in a couple of hours or so."

He left by the back door, and Dani made a dash for the front. She could skirt around the house and catch sight of him before he disappeared into the bayou, if that's where he was going. On the other hand, if he was going to the garage to get a car, she was dead.

She tried not to look as if she was in a race as she crossed the gallery and headed for the lawn. Coming around the corner to the rear of the house, she paused and looked at the overgrown garden. The boxwood hedges were in desperate need of trimming, the limbs of the rosebushes were so long and gnarled that they twisted about one another, and in the center of the lawn the wisteria that Dani suspected had once draped gracefully over the arched gazebo, now almost engulfed it.

She fidgeted nervously, afraid to step into the open to look for him, and afraid he'd already gone. Then she saw him beyond the gazebo. He was moving into the shadows at the edge of the lawn. Dani made her way through the overgrown gardens, then paused at the gazebo to make certain he hadn't seen her. Satisfied, she took a deep breath and stepped onto the path that led in the direction Anton had taken.

Sanitee stepped from the other side of the gazebo and into her way. "Oh, excuse me, Miss Lane," she said, smiling. "I'm sorry, I didn't mean to step into your way. Isn't it a beautiful day, though? I think I must get a basket and pick some wildflowers for the table."

Dani looked into Sanitee's green eyes and knew instantly that stepping into her way had been exactly what the woman had intended. She glanced past the housekeeper's shoulder and saw that Anton was nowhere in sight. Dani smiled. "Yes, it is a beautiful day. That's why I came out, to enjoy a little more sunshine and fresh air after being cooped up in the office all afternoon."

"Well, don't leave the immediate gardens," Sanitee said. Her eyes seemed suddenly shuttered. "It's not really . . . safe . . . out there, if you don't know your way around."

Dani nodded, wondering with a sense of unease if the woman's words were a veiled threat or merely those of friendly caution. Anton was gone. The sun was already low in the sky and throwing shadows everywhere. There was still enough daylight left to try and find Anton, but she didn't relish going into the bayou alone, especially not after their ride that morning had proven to her how easily she could lose all sense of direction. "Sanitee, why is it that Mr. Reichard doesn't take care of the gardens anymore? They must have been quite beautiful."

She saw the other woman stiffen at her question.

"The garden was his mama's pride and joy. Having it perfect, the way she kept it, would only remind him of her."

Dani watched her walk away, then looked back at the spot where Anton had disappeared into the bayou. For a brief, reckless moment she thought of going after him in spite of her apprehension, then shrugged the idea away. She was a city girl, and getting lost in the bayou was not her idea of fun.

Moments later she returned to the house, feeling frustrated and momentarily beaten, then she remembered the fax Anton had sent. If she was lucky, he'd thrown it into the wastebasket. At the very least the confirmation slip the machine spit out would tell her what number he'd called.

She dashed to his office and went directly to the long table that the fax and copy machines sat on. The wastebasket was empty, but the confirmation slip was still in the machine. She pulled it out and looked at the number. It didn't belong to either Carter or Floyd. Folding the small slip of paper, she tucked it into her pocket.

Dani glanced at the file cabinets, then decided against trying to go through them again. Sanitee was somewhere around, and the woman had an uncanny way of popping up where she was least expected. She left the office and made her way upstairs to her room, noting that if Sanitee was about, she was being as silent as a church mouse, which made Dani nervous. She'd much rather hear the housekeeper clanging pots and pans together in the kitchen. At least that way she'd know where the woman was. Dani retrieved her cellular phone and dialed Stan's number.

"Yeah?" he growled into the line.

"Stan, this is Dani."

"Rescue call already?"

"No. I need you to check out a number for me. Find out who it belongs to." She rattled off the fax number. "It's a fax number Anton used today, but I don't know whose it is. He sent me out of the room when he used it. I'll call you back tomorrow."

"Sounds interesting, kid. Know what it was that he sent?"

"No." She hung up before he could ask her any more questions she couldn't answer. Dani tucked the phone back into her suitcase and was about to open the armoire and decide on what to change into for dinner when she heard the unmistakable sound of car tires rolling over the crushed oyster-shell drive. She walked to the open French doors and, crossing the gallery, looked down at the long black car that had pulled to a stop before the entry.

Floyd Pellichet climbed from the vehicle and, slamming his door, walked toward the house.

If the set of his shoulders was any indication, Dani guessed that Floyd was not a happy man.

SIX

Dani met Floyd at the bottom of the stairs.

"Where's Anton?" he demanded.

She shrugged. "Wherever it is he goes every day after four o'clock."

"Sanitee," Floyd yelled, his voice filling the foyer and reverberating off its walls. The quiet and polite demeanor he'd affected during their interview was nowhere in evidence. His face was flushed, his manner agitated.

The housekeeper came through the swinging door that led to the kitchen and glared at Floyd Pellichet. The black braid coiled atop her crown danced with reflection of the setting sun's light that streamed into the room through the windows.

"Where's Anton?" he demanded again.

"Out," she said haughtily, green eyes cool and challenging.

"I know he's out, dammit, but I need to talk to him, so where is he?"

"Out," she said again. She glanced at the grandfather

clock. "He'll be back in two hours. Maybe less." She turned back to the kitchen and, putting a hand on the door to push it open, glanced over her shoulder at Floyd and, with a wry smile, murmured, "Maybe more."

"Damned woman," Floyd said, as she disappeared back into the kitchen. "Disrespectful and arrogant. Acts as if she's the owner of the place instead of the damned maid."

At that moment Dani heard the screen door in the rear of the house slam closed, and turned toward the end of the foyer to stare at the swinging door that led to the kitchen.

Floyd heard it too. "Was that Anton?"

She wanted to say, *How should I know?* Instead she walked to the door and pushed it open. She had taken an instant and most unreasonable dislike to Jessica Beausoil, and she was quickly coming to dislike Floyd Pellichet too.

Anton was getting a carton of milk from the refrigerator and looked up as the door swung open. He saw Floyd standing behind Dani. "Floyd, what are you doing here?"

The tall attorney stalked into the kitchen. "I need to talk to you. It's important."

Anton straightened, slipping the milk into the same canvas sack Dani had seen Sanitee give him earlier. "Sorry, but it'll have to wait. I've got to go back out for a while."

"I don't think you understand, Anton," Floyd snapped. "It's important."

"So is this," Anton said, his tone holding an intimation of menace so dark, it caused Dani to actually grip the doorjamb in surprise.

"Someone tried to hack into my files on the venture."

Dani saw Anton's shoulders stiffen beneath the white shirt he wore. He had half turned toward the door, but now swung back to look at Floyd. "Stay and we'll talk when I get back, Floyd. Or come out in the morning. Whichever. But I can't stand here and discuss this now."

"Anton, dammit, this can't wait," Floyd said, impatience lacing each word.

Anton stared at Floyd, his gaze hard and unyielding. "It will have to." He looked at Dani. "Do you know anything about hacking?"

She frowned. Was he asking her if she was the one who'd tried to get into Floyd's computer files?

"About tracking them down?" he added at her look of puzzlement.

She shook her head. "Not really."

He screwed his face into a sneer of resignation at her lack of helpfulness and looked back at Floyd. "Did they get in?"

"No," Floyd said. "I don't think so."

"Then we'll talk when I get back."

Before Pellichet could say anything further, Anton slammed past the screen door, letting it crash closed behind him.

"I don't have time to sit around here and twiddle my thumbs waiting for him to do heaven only knows what," Floyd snapped. He glanced at Sanitee, who had busied herself at the stove. "What's he do out there every day, anyway? Where does he go?"

The housekeeper shrugged. "You want to know his business, you ask him."

Floyd glowered at her, anger shading his cheeks purple. He turned to Dani. "Tell him we'll talk in the morning. I'm going back to the office to see if I can figure out what in the hell is going on and put a stop to it."

She nodded and followed him to the front door, waiting until his car was well down the drive before going upstairs. Grabbing her cellular phone, she dialed Stan's number. "Please, please let him still be there," she mumbled as the phone rang in her ear.

"Yeah, what?" he growled into the receiver after the tenth ring.

"Stan, it's Dani."

"If you're calling for a rescue, kid, you'll have to wait. We've got a problem here. One of our couriers just got shot, and the police are all over the place asking questions. They catch this guy, I hope they string him up and . . ."

"Is he . . . the courier . . . dead?" she asked, praying Stan would say no.

"No. The doc said it was serious, but he'd pull through."

Dani nodded, thankful. It wasn't even safe for a kid to deliver papers anymore. "I need you to check something, Stan."

"Tomorrow," he said.

"Okay, but first thing in the morning. See what you can find out about Floyd Pellichet's personal finances. And find out what kind of computer system he has in his office."

"Computer system?"

"Yes. And find me a hacker. A good one. The best. I'll call you tomorrow."

Dani hung up and tucked the phone back into her bag. Someone wanted into Floyd's computer files, and she wanted to know why. Glancing at her watch, she decided she might as well start dressing for dinner. She peeled off her jeans and walked to the tall armoire. A yawn gripped her halfway across the room, and she paused to stretch. She hadn't gotten much sleep the previous night, and she didn't think she should risk another late-night sneak peek at Anton's files this soon. He might be waiting to see if that's what she was going to do. So tonight she would sleep. But first she had to get through dinner.

Dani pulled the armoire's ornate cherrywood door open, and a massive flash of black leapt out at her. She screamed at the top of her lungs and threw herself away from whatever it was that had lunged toward her. A hot jab of pain shot up her calf as her ankle turned beneath her, and she fell to the floor. With her heart racing in fear and her scream still echoing about her, Dani twisted around to confront the apparition who'd flown at her from the closet.

Nothing was there.

Anxious, she pushed herself up to a sitting position and, still searching the room with a wary gaze, rubbed at her aching ankle.

The door to her room suddenly opened and, as it did, Pichouette raced from beneath Dani's bed, past the door, and into the hallway.

"Are you all right, Miss Lane?" Sanitee appeared in the doorway and headed across the room to kneel beside Dani. "I was in the foyer and thought I heard you scream."

Dani stared into the hall where Pichouette had escaped, then looked up at the housekeeper. She hadn't seen Sanitee when the door had opened, but she had seen the cat run out and the housekeeper appear a second later. And Sanitee had green eyes, just like Pichouette.

"Miss Lane, are you all right?" the housekeeper asked again.

Dani shook her head, almost laughing at the outrageous thought. Obviously the cat had given her a fright so bad, it had not only caused her to twist her ankle, but had also affected her brain. She took Sanitee's offered arm and leaned on her as she rose to her feet. "I . . . the cat startled me, that's all." She took a tentative step, putting as little pressure as possible on the injured ankle. It hurt, but the pain was bearable. "I didn't know she was in the armoire." She looked at Sanitee, about to ask her for an ice pack, but changed her mind. If she did that, the housekeeper would tell Anton she was hurt, and for some insane reason she didn't want him to know that his cat had scared her again. If she made nothing of the incident, maybe Sanitee wouldn't mention it. "I'll be fine, Sanitee, thank you."

The housekeeper nodded and left the room.

For the next ten minutes Dani sat with her foot in the bathroom basin, cold water pouring over her ankle. By the time she was done her toes were freezing and her ankle was numb, but at least she could walk without too much of a limp. She wondered how many lives Pichouette had used up, then thought that, as far as she was concerned, it probably wasn't enough.

Walking back into the bedroom to dress, she again moved to the armoire, though this time more warily. Once certain the cat hadn't returned, Dani relaxed and chose a dress of royal-blue moiré silk. Its luminous threads brought out the gold-red highlights in her hair, and the intense color accentuated her eyes. At least by emphasizing those she might avert Anton's attention from her slightly swollen ankle and the limp that went along with it.

Out of the corner of his eye Anton spotted Pichouette sauntering through the foyer. "So, Miss Lane," he said, turning his gaze to hers and tapping a finger absently against the crystal wineglass beside his dinner plate, "I understand you had an accident this afternoon."

Dani clenched a hand under the table. She'd hoped the housekeeper wouldn't tell him. So much for hope. Forcing a smile to her lips, she met his gaze and felt its instant pull. It was like looking into an infinite chasm that threatened to reach out, clutch her within its grasp, and pull her deep into its endlessness. But it was too late to look away, even if she'd wanted to. "The . . . your cat just startled me, that's all. I . . ." She felt warmth flood her entire body, and with it a yearning she didn't understand. "I didn't expect her to be in the armoire."

He frowned. "Neither would I, but she always has liked to curl up in out-of-the-way places. She was my sister's cat, and always slept in her room. The one next to yours. Pichouette is old and, I suppose, misses Sherry."

Dani saw the darkness that invaded his eyes at the mention of his sister but remained quiet.

"Perhaps Pichouette merely got confused and went into the wrong room, or thought she could get to Sherry's room through yours. In any case, I'd suggest you not leave the door to your room, or that of the armoire, open from now on."

Dani didn't bother to tell him that she hadn't left either door open, but that only allowed three possibilities: That the cat knew how to open doors herself, which was ridiculous; that Sanitee had put the cat into Dani's closet, which was also ridiculous since the housekeeper had no reason to do that; or that Pichouette had merely followed Dani into the room earlier and she hadn't noticed.

The last was the most logical answer. So why did she have doubts about it?

Anton sipped slowly at his wine, then set the glass back on the table and looked long and hard at Dani. "I had a few friends who went to USL," he said, totally startling her. "Right around the same time as you."

She stared at him, her heart suddenly surrounded by an icy layer of fear. Somehow she knew this was not merely idle conversation. "Really?" she finally managed through the knot that had twisted her throat and was threatening to cut off her air supply.

"Jessica was one of them," Anton said. "In fact"—his eyes bored into Dani's, as if daring her to continue with her lie—"I mentioned to her that you'd gone there, but she couldn't remember having met you." He let the words hang in the air between them, their implication clear.

Dani's mind raced in search of a response. "I, um . . ." She smiled. "Actually, I don't remember meeting her either. Maybe we didn't have any classes together."

A deriding smile pulled at his lips. She remembered

having noted that same smile on his face in one of the newspaper photos she'd seen while researching him.

"I find it hard to believe that anyone attending USL at the time Jessica was there wouldn't remember her. She's not an easy person to forget."

Dani was surprised at the stab of jealousy his comments about Jessica Beausoil brought on as she wondered if *he* was the one who was finding the woman "not an easy person to forget." "Oh, I remember her," Dani said, telling herself she was being ridiculous again, "I just meant I don't remember ever having met her."

He nodded, but she could see that her answer hadn't satisfied him. Dani had a sinking feeling that when Anton's former fiancée had told him that she didn't remember Dani Lane from USL, suspicions had erupted within him that weren't going to be vanquished easily.

"How about Beau Hammond?" Anton said.

Dani stared at him blankly. She'd heard the name, knew she should recognize it, but her mind had inexplicably shut off, refusing to give her even the tiniest tidbit of information. "Beau Hammond," she repeated thoughtfully.

"Quarterback on the football team the year you graduated," Anton offered. "Took USL to the all-state finals. Married the homecoming queen the same night as the last game. Surely you remember him?"

The doorbell chimed, and Dani looked toward the foyer, hoping she'd been saved by the bell. He could be making idle conversation, or he could be weaving a lie to test her, she wasn't sure. And she hadn't the faintest idea who Beau Hammond was.

When she looked back Anton was staring at her, his gaze cold and hard, as if he'd read her thoughts.

"Tony," Carter said, walking into the room. "Mind telling me what's so important that I had to break a date to come out here tonight?"

Anton's dark brows rose slightly. "A date, Carter?" He glanced at Sanitee, who had entered to clear their plates from the table.

Dani noticed the look and remembered having seen the housekeeper sneaking out to meet someone in the garden the night before. She suddenly wondered if Anton had seen her too, and for some reason suspected her midnight lover was Carter?

"Or another of your Bourbon Street strippers?" Anton added.

Dani watched Sanitee for a reaction to Anton's words, but the woman showed none.

Carter shrugged. "To each his own." He smiled a hello at Dani.

She returned the acknowledgment, and he directed his attention back to Anton. "So, what's up?"

Anton rose. "I have something to discuss with you." He glanced back at Dani. "I won't need you in on this, Miss Lane," he said curtly, then turned to Sanitee. "Please bring Carter and me some coffee in my study."

Dani sipped at her wine and watched them leave the dining room. She'd have to wait until after Sanitee took Anton his coffee before she could slip into her own office. By then, however, they might be through talking about whatever it was Anton thought was so important it couldn't wait until morning, but she'd have to take that chance.

Picking up the wineglass, Dani walked into the foyer and stood beside the front door, looking out at the night through one of the slender windows that framed the entry door. Beyond the gallery was nothing but dark shadows, fractured here and there by pale splits of moonlight.

She was about to turn away, deciding that more than enough time had elapsed so that she could go to her office without being seen by Sanitee, when a movement in the gardens beyond the drive caught her eye. Dani flicked off the foyer's chandelier and, opening the front door, stepped out onto the gallery.

Dressed in the same flowing black gown that she had worn when Dani had seen her the previous night, the woman Dani assumed was Sanitee moved around one of the tall oaks in the distance that lined the drive and disappeared into the shadows.

"I don't care how well you checked her out, Carter," Anton said with a snarl, "you didn't do a good enough job."

"Tony, I . . ."

"She didn't go to USL, Carter. She lied, and if she lied about that, what the hell else did she lie about? Her name maybe? The dead husband and child? Maybe even that she's a secretary?"

"I told you she didn't have any experience, Tony," Carter said. "And it wasn't as if we exactly had a bevy of eager applicants to choose from."

Anton slammed his hands down on his desk and leaned across it to glare at Carter. "I don't care that she doesn't have experience, Carter. I don't even care that she lied about USL, if it's the only lie. But I do care if she's not who, and possibly what, she says she is. Do you understand?" A thin blue vein pulsed madly upon the side of his neck as his jaw clenched. "Do you know how much damage she could do if she was sent here by our competitors, Carter? By Eldon or Stuart?"

"What could they hope to do by sending a woman in here?"

Anton's hands curled into fists. He hadn't been so mad since . . . He shrugged the thought aside, not wanting to think about the last time he'd been so angry, because it had been at himself. Almost three years earlier, when he'd regained consciousness in the hospital and the doctors had told him what had happened, what he'd done. The rage had nearly consumed him. Finally, after being restrained, drugged, and counseled for weeks on end, he'd gotten it under control and had begun learning to live with the reality his recklessness had wrought. But the pain and anger had never really gone away, he'd just managed to live with them, burying them deep inside of him, except during the dead of night, when they resurfaced to keep him from sleep.

"She has access to my office, Carter," Anton said slowly, his tone dripping acid. "My files, architectural drawings, loan papers, expenditures, computer records. In other words, everything connected with the River Queen."

"The River Queen is too far ahead of both Eldon's and Stuart's projects for it to matter, Tony," Carter said. "Anyway, if they'd sent her here and it was discovered, the city could yank their licenses."

"*If* it was discovered," Anton snapped.

"I didn't find out anything that connected her to either of them."

"You didn't find out she didn't attend USL either."

Carter sighed. "You want me to fire her?"

"No. It just might be that graduating from USL is the only thing she lied about, and if that's the case, I don't care. But I want you to check her out again, Carter, and this time find out everything down to the damned second the woman was born."

"Okay, but I don't think there's anything to worry about."

"Nothing to worry about?" Anton stared at Carter as if he'd lost his mind. "The games manufacturers have just asked for another extension on their delivery date, the contractors are gouging the hell out of us, the artist who was commissioned to paint the lobby murals has been sick in bed with the flu for two weeks, and every day we run past our scheduled opening will cost us thousands."

"Tony, I know—"

"The bank is expecting a report on our status before they hand over any more money, and if one more thing goes wrong, I don't see them doing that, Carter. Do you?"

"Tony, I—"

"I see them pulling the plug, Carter," Anton snapped, cutting the attorney off, "and I'm not prepared to pick up the total note myself, which means quite a few people are going to go a hell of a lot further down the tubes than I will."

"I'll take care of it." Carter edged toward the door.

"And one other thing, Carter," Anton said. "Just so you know, I was going over some of the contractor numbers for the Queen today, and several didn't look right. I faxed them to Beau to check out."

"Didn't look right," Carter repeated. He nodded "Good. Good. If something's wrong, Beau will find it."

"That's what I'm counting on."

Dani stood frozen beside the door that led from her office into Anton's. He knew. The knowledge pounded in her brain as her heart hammered frantically against her breast. He knew she'd lied. She ran to her desk and reached for the phone, then snatched her hand back. If she used the office phone, he might see the extension light go on, and then he'd know she was there, know she had overheard him.

But did it matter? a voice in the back of her mind screamed. Maybe he already knew she was there. Maybe everything she'd overheard was for her benefit. She stood motionless, unable to decide what to do. If she left the office now, she might run into him in the foyer as Carter was leaving. If she didn't leave now, he might come in there for some reason. She hurried to the door that led into the foyer, then turned and walked back to the one that adjoined the two offices. The two men were still talking, calmer now, their voices lower.

Dani returned to the outer door and stepped into the foyer, half expecting to be confronted by Sanitee, then breathing a sigh of relief at remembering she'd seen the woman slip from the house earlier. She closed the office door softly behind her and turned toward the stairs.

"Miss Lane."

Startled, Dani whirled and stared into Sanitee's green eyes.

"I just brought Anton and Mr. Tyrene more coffee." She smiled. "Would you like some?"

SEVEN

Dani kicked her shoes off, unzipped the blue moiré silk dress, and shrugged it from her shoulders. For all the good it had done her she might as well have worn burlap. She tossed the dress onto a chair and frowned. She'd seen Sanitee leave the house dressed in a long flowing gown of black. Yet only minutes later the housekeeper had stood in the foyer, wearing the same dark green dress that she'd served dinner in?

She sat on the bed, absently running a hand over the coverlet, then looked down at something soft balled up under her finger. Cat hair. Black cat hair. Dani glanced at the armoire and remembered her last encounter with Pichouette. A woman in a black gown had run across the lawn. A black cat had lunged at Dani from the armoire. Sanitee had green eyes that sent a chill through Dani. Pichouette had green eyes that gazed upon Dani with seemingly haughty contempt.

Dani shot up off the bed as a preposterous thought zipped through her mind. "Right. Cat people," she snapped irritably at herself. "Let Stan hear that one, Dani, and he'll have you writing the comic section."

Dani picked up the dress and walked toward the armoire, stopping several feet short of reaching it. She stared at the large closet. It couldn't happen twice, she told herself. Nevertheless, instead of proceeding to hang the dress up, she turned away and threw it back onto the chair.

She had a story to get, and if she wanted it, she'd better start concentrating on the real problem at hand: Anton knew she'd lied. Her hands trembled. She walked into the bathroom and turned on the shower. If he was going to confront her with the fact, why hadn't he done it earlier, while they'd dined? She wished she had been able to overhear his conversation with Carter from the beginning.

Removing her underthings and dropping them into the hamper basket next to the sink, Dani stepped into the shower and instantly relaxed beneath the pelting hot water as it rushed over her skin.

A soft thud, seeming to come from the bedroom, caused her to pause in the midst of shampooing her hair. She drew the shower curtain aside and peeked out. "Hello?" Steam drifted from the bathroom in a swirl, floating out through the open door and into the bedroom. She never closed the bathroom door while showering because she hated the sound of overhead fans in most modern bathrooms. But she hated how the steam fogged up mirrors and everything else in the room even more, so she always left the door open.

"Hello?" she called again when no one answered. "I'm in the shower." She'd been careful to shut the bedroom door and was certain Pichouette hadn't followed her into the room. Most likely it was Sanitee bringing her towels or coffee or something.

Dani stood still and waited, but no one answered her call and no further sound met her ears. She went back to lathering her hair. Obviously she was wrong. The sound had probably come from elsewhere in the house, if she'd actually heard something at all. Maybe it had been a knock in the pipes. This was an old house.

Sanitee stood at one of the parlor windows and watched the taillights of Carter's car move down the drive. She was worried. When the small spots of red finally disappeared from view, she turned from the window and walked to the door of Anton's study. "Would you like some more coffee?" she asked quietly.

He was hunched over his desk, flipping through the pages of a large spreadsheet and scribbling numbers onto a scratch pad. She watched him for several seconds before he looked up. "No, thanks, Sanitee, but you can lock up now."

As she closed his door she glanced up the staircase toward the second floor landing. She had heard the faint hum of the shower pipes turn off a good ten minutes ago.

Suddenly a scream split the quietness, echoing down the hallways and resounding off the walls, only to be followed by another.

Anton jerked open the door of his study. "What the hell?" He looked around wildly, then followed Sanitee's gaze to the second-floor landing. Pushing past her, he charged up the stairs, his long legs taking them two at a time with ease. "Dani," he yelled, and ran down the hall to her door.

He grabbed the S-shaped silver handle and pushed down. It refused to give, which meant the door was locked. "Dani?" Anton slammed a fist against a white panel of the door. "Dani? Let me in. What's wrong?" He pounded on the door again. "Answer me. Dani?"

Another scream nearly shattered his nerves. "Dani, dammit, open the door."

"Here, use this," Sanitee said quietly, moving to stand at his side. She held out a key.

He grabbed it, rammed the small reed of silver into the lock, twisted it with a jerk, and shoved the door open. Anton lunged into the room. "Dani?"

She was huddled on top of the dressing table, covered by nothing but a towel. Her hair was pinned atop her head in a coiled knot that had come slightly askew, allowing several long tendrils to fall across her shoulders, and her eyes were as big and wide as tennis balls.

Anton rushed to her, grabbing her arms and twisting her around so that she was forced to look at him. "What's wrong?" he demanded.

She was trembling violently.

"Dani?" He shook her. "What's wrong?"

She looked up at him then, wild- and glassy-eyed, lips quivering, hands shaking, and opened her mouth to scream again.

Anton tightened his grasp on her arms. "No, it's okay. I'm here. Now what's wrong?"

He saw her focus then, and a shudder ripped through her body as she looked past him.

"There's a . . . there's a . . ."

"What?" Anton demanded. "What?"

"In . . . the . . . bed," she said, her voice little more than a garbled whisper. "There's a . . . a . . ." She pointed a shaking finger toward the canopy bed.

He turned and took a step in the direction she indicated.

"No," Dani screamed. "Don't!"

He stopped and looked back, puzzled.

"There's a . . . sn . . . a . . . snake," she finally managed.

Anton's gaze darted between Dani and Sanitee. "Snake?" he repeated. "In here?"

She nodded frantically, her entire body shaking. "In . . . in my bed."

Anton walked to the fireplace and picked up a brass poker, then turned back. He glanced at the soft glowing lamp on the night table. "Turn the overhead light on, Sanitee," he said over his shoulder.

The chandelier flickered into brightness, filling the room with light.

Anton cautiously approached the left side of the bed, the poker gripped solidly in one fist. Movement beneath one of the pillows drew his eye, and he paused, his body tensing as he saw the side of the reptile's body and recognized the black, yellow, and orange rings of a deadly coral snake. He waited for the reptile to either settle or move farther into view, readying to strike. It stilled, only the tip of its tail remaining visible from beneath the pillow. Anton reached out, slipped the end of the poker under one corner of the pillow, and flipped it aside, instantly swinging the poker back up in readiness to strike.

He brought the poker back down with all the force his arm had. The snake moved, slightly, and just before the poker would have struck him a deadly blow, Anton's eyes widened in shock and he swerved his arm to the side. The poker slammed into the blankets with a dull thud, sending them flying upward and causing the mattress beneath to bounce.

Dani screamed.

Anton dropped the poker instantly and, bending, scooped the snake up into his hands. He held the reptile so that his head was only a few inches from Anton's face. "Clyde," he said, *"bon Dieu,* how in the hell did you get in here, little friend?"

Dani stared, unable to believe what she was seeing, what was happening. The man was caressing a snake!

Sanitee hurried across the room to peer around Anton's shoulder. "One of yours?" she asked softly, looking up at him with a frown of worry.

Anton nodded and cradled the snake against his chest. He turned back to Dani. "He couldn't have hurt you."

"It's . . . it's a . . . snake. It's . . ." She swallowed hard, unable to believe the creature had been in her bed, that Anton was holding it in his arms as if it were a kitten.

"He's helpless," Anton said, rubbing a thumb tenderly over the back of the snake's head. "Corals are poisonous, but Clyde doesn't have any fangs, and he can't slither around too good because his back was broken. He has no control over his last half. Believe me, Clyde was probably more afraid of you than you were of him."

Dani remained huddled on the dressing table, her fear still very much in control. Snakes were icky, crawly, slithering primitive creatures that were pure danger.

"Dani," Anton said, his voice cutting through her fearful thoughts, "Clyde can't hurt you."

She stared at the reptile. It had a name? She found a snake having a name almost ludicrous.

"Should I take him?" Sanitee said, holding out her hands. "There's a box in the pantry."

Anton looked at the housekeeper, a coldness coming into his eyes that Dani saw but didn't understand. "No. I'll take care of him. You lock the house and go on to bed."

She nodded and silently left the room.

He looked back at Dani. "You don't have to stay up on that dressing table."

She shuddered again, chilled at just the prospect of being near a snake.

As if summoned by Dani's thoughts, Pichouette sauntered quietly into the room. She walked directly to Anton and began doing figure eights around his legs, rubbing her large body against his pant legs and purring loudly, her eyes closed as if she were in ecstasy.

Dani glared down at the cat and figured all she needed now were a few monstrous spiders to trot across the carpet, and she'd have every excuse in the world to go completely crazy.

Anton ushered Pichouette from the room and turned back to Dani. "I don't know how Clyde got into your bed," he said softly, though she heard an undercurrent of anger to his tone, "but I'll find out, because it wasn't by himself."

Dani stared at the coiled snake.

Anton began to step into the hallway, but glanced back and saw that Dani had still made no move to dislodge herself from the top of the dressing table. She was staring at the bed now, as if afraid another creature hid beneath the rumpled folds of the sheets, waiting to swallow her whole. He knew how gripping that kind of un-reasonable fear could be, the kind that stemmed from the threat that things were out of your control, that your life, in the blink of an instant, could be changed forever, and you had no choice in the matter.

Anton walked over to the bed. Holding Clyde against his body with one hand, he grabbed the edges of the coverlet and sheet with the other and ripped them away from the bed. "Nothing else there," he said, looking back at Dani. "No cats, no snakes, no monsters. Nothing." He smiled. "I think you're pretty well safe for the night."

Dani nodded and tried to return the smile.

Anton stared at her, seeing the fear that still lingered on her features, but he saw something else too, something in her that stirred all the old desires, all the old wants. He sensed that she wasn't a woman easily fright-ened, or one who gave up on something she truly wanted. She was strong and independent, but like *the others*, there was a wounded quality about her. He felt an urge to take her into his arms, to shield her from the world, to protect her. That thought and image no sooner came into his mind than another replaced it, one much more sensual, much more seductive . . . more personal. He wanted to hold her, but not only to protect her. Almost from the first moment he'd seen her, he had wanted, needed, to feel her body pressed to his, hot with the same need and want she stirred within him.

Anton mentally slapped the thought away, incensed with himself for harboring it in the first place. He had nothing left to offer a woman, nothing left inside of himself to offer anyone. And it was better that way. No more than he deserved.

His thoughts were interrupted when he saw another shudder rack her body and heard a small sob escape Dani's lips. Her gaze was still glued, as if hypnotically, to the snake, and he realized that even though he'd tried to reassure her about Clyde, the continued sight of him was feeding her fear. Stroking the snake's head, Anton stepped out into the hall and placed the half-coiled Clyde on a nearby table. "Stay there, *mon ami*, until I come back for you."

Clyde tried to snuggle himself next to the vase that sat on the table, but the last half of his body merely hung off the table, limp and lifeless.

Anton gently lifted Clyde's lower body and curled it onto the table for him. "There you go, *mon'tite ami*. Rest easy for a while now." He looked about for Pichouette and saw the cat sitting a few feet away, preening. "Guard him, *ma petite*, until I get back."

The cat meowed and pranced over to settle beneath the small table. Anton stepped back into Dani's room.

She was still sitting huddled on the dressing table.

He moved to stand in front of her and encircled her upper arms with his large hands. Her flesh was as cold as ice, and fear still glistened within the blue of her eyes. "Are you all right?" he asked, looking down at her. There was a catch in his throat that he didn't want to feel.

She trembled. "I . . . think so," she said shakily. She hesitated as she clutched the towel around her breasts and stepped down from her perch on the table. His gaze caught and held hers, and as Dani stared into his eyes she saw them turn darker, until the blue-gray mists were as black as the blackest night, and roiling with emotion.

She couldn't read the surfeit of emotions she saw jousting for control within those dark, infinite depths, though she sensed what they were and could feel the battle he fought against surrendering to them. She knew what he was feeling, what he was trying to deny, trying to ignore, because she felt it too. For this moment, this brief millisecond in time, he wanted her . . . and she wanted him. Dani tilted her chin upward, giving in to the desire to be touched by him.

Anton found himself suddenly pierced by those dazzling dark blue eyes, eyes that unexpectedly reached inside of him and touched something that hadn't been touched in a very long time. The heat of mutual attraction danced between them like flames upon dry kindling, threatening to erupt into an inferno neither would be able to control or deny.

Her face was all too near his own, the fresh scent of her skin, her hair, the lavender cologne she'd sprayed on after her shower. The melding fragrances hovered in the air between them, teasing his senses as the fever of need invaded his blood and rushed through him, overcoming all the resolves and vows of the past three years. Desire mocked his self-control, making a travesty of the thin threads of restraint he tried to hold on to. Hunger erupted deep down inside of him, a feeling both comfortably familiar and strangely new. It wrapped around him like a coil of hope, reaching through the shroud of loneliness he'd lived in for so long and offering a spark of warmth.

Anton struggled to resist it, and he could have, if he hadn't looked into her eyes again and seen the same want that he felt, the same need reflected there. His hands tightened their hold on her. A groan of defeat tore through his throat, stilling his hesitant thoughts, weakening his resolve further, and Anton forgot everything but the beckoning of her lips as he drew her toward him, pulling her body against his. The hunger in him was too desperate to ignore, too intense to deny, and he was both astounded by his surrender to it, and oblivious of it. Pleasure, ecstasy, need, hunger—like nothing he had known for three years—overwhelmed him and fused with the raw fury he felt at the defeat of his defenses. The combination made his kiss a ruthless assault that plundered, sought, and took.

He had kissed her once before, but this time was different, this time he felt his defenses crumbling, his barriers against emotion, against love, feeling, and warmth, falling aside. And there was nothing he could do to stop it, nothing he wanted to do. The world exploded around him, the air crackling from the heat of the flames that threatened to devour his body in a maelstrom of rapture he was powerless to resist. Emotions he'd thought would never surface again surged through him, refusing to be either controlled or denied.

She was not who she claimed to be, could possibly have been sent here to destroy him. He knew that, understood that, but logic for the moment had lost out to the mutinous demands of his body. She was available to him and forbidden to him, and Anton was finding the combination an irresistible allure that only served to deepen the feral, rudimentary hunger that had seized every cell within his body.

His tongue danced around hers. He had remained strong, resistant, alone for almost one thousand days, losing himself in the daily chores and challenges of business and telling himself he neither wanted nor needed anything else. And he had been wrong. He crushed his mouth to hers, joyful and angry, hating himself, hating her for being there for him, making him want her. In the back of his mind he wished fervently that she would push him away, but everything else within him prayed that she would not.

His prayers were answered when he felt her own tongue move around his, tentatively exploring, unconsciously teasing, even while her body, still stiff within the circle of his arms, silently conveyed her inclination to flee.

He drew her tighter into his arms, deepening his kiss, pressing his hands to the bare flesh of her back, reveling in its softness, its warmth. The swell of his arousal pressed against her, and a moan of longing rumbled from his throat, meeting, melding that which slipped quietly and softly from her own.

She twisted slightly in his embrace, and the towel fell to the floor.

Dani couldn't breathe. Her heart was pounding furiously in her throat and a burning, searing heat like none she had ever felt before had erupted somewhere deep inside of her. It raced through her veins like a volcanic force that, with each passing second, was growing more profound. The sensation fought for control of her fear, pushing it aside and forcing her to wonder why she had been afraid of him, why she had been afraid of anything.

Anton's kiss deepened. He drew her even closer, pressing her breasts into the soft fabric of his shirt, crushing her against him until there was no space, no shadow, no light separating their bodies from each other. She could feel every hard plane and line of him molded against her, passion fusing two bodies to one as it met, touched, drew, and conquered them.

She trembled as his hands moved over her bare flesh, and she felt her heart beat faster, faster, her breath turning ragged, her pulse racing. Dani knew she should pull away from him. He was not the kind of man she wanted in her life. He was darkness, she preferred the light. He harbored secrets, she yearned for closeness and trust. He demanded honesty, she had come to him in deception.

His lips ravaged hers. Reality fused with fantasy, and suddenly all of her yesterdays and tomorrows disappeared, forgotten, as only this day, this moment, existed. He was wrong for her, they were wrong for each other, but she couldn't pull away from him, couldn't let go of the one man she knew she had been waiting for all of her life.

Anton tried to fight the feelings welling up inside of him, but it did no good. He wanted her, had wanted her from the moment he'd seen her, and had been unable to make the yearning go away, no matter how much he'd fought it. It wasn't who she really was, or why she was really at Bayou Noir that was a danger to him, the ultimate threat was merely her. Deep down inside, he'd known that. She had looked at him, and the barriers he'd built around his emotions had begun to crumble like so much dust in the wind. He'd fought it, denied it, but raw loneliness, ignored for so long, refused to be ignored any longer.

He'd felt her slight resistance at the first touch of his lips to hers, sensed her reluctance, even her fear, but he hadn't released her, because he'd wanted, needed to ignite the same fires of desire in her that burned so hot within himself.

Dani didn't want to respond to him. She was here on business, here to get a story, here only to further her career. But at the moment, none of those arguments seemed to matter, or give her the strength to pull away from him. Everything she thought she'd wanted, needed in her life was forgotten as her mouth and body responded to his. He was a stranger, and yet she felt as if she'd known him, been waiting for him, all of her life. His lips were both hard and soft against her own, his tongue unrelenting as it reached hungrily into her mouth, exploring, seducing, loving, and stoking fires everywhere within her.

She felt one of his hands slide down the curve of her back, move up over the swell of her hip, and caress her breast. Every thought but that of the man who held her in his embrace slipped from her mind. Like thunder rolling over a prairie, desire rolled through her body, an onslaught that was at once mercilessly fierce and surprisingly gentle. Needy pleasure coiled hot and tight deep within the core of her, while want and desire tugged at her senses, tingled her nerves, teased her flesh.

He moved his mouth from hers and lightly ran the tip of his tongue over the curve of her cheekbone, along the line of her jaw, and the column of her neck. Bending, his tongue flicked the taut peak of her nipple.

A soft meow from the hallway was the only sound that broke the silence—but it was enough.

Dani wrenched away from him, gasping deeply for breath, her heart slamming against her breast, eyes wide as she stared up at him. "No," she whispered finally, and shook her head, "we can't."

Anton stared at her for a long moment as desire, need, and tenderness slipped away from him and the long-harbored anger poured back, chilling both his heart and his soul. He saw her lips tremble as she met his gaze, saw the dismay that came into them at what had happened between them and her realization that she stood before him naked. She scooped up the towel that had fallen to the floor and tried to cover herself. He watched as she backed away from him as if afraid, and Anton felt her rejection like a knife piercing his soul.

He stiffened, all emotion leaving his face. One dark brow arched skyward. "Obviously," Anton said, his voice cold and harsh now, "I owe you another apology." Turning abruptly, he strode from the room, leaving Dani to stare after him, her body still hot and tight with desire.

EIGHT

The next morning Dani's snooze alarm sounded, then automatically shut off. She knew she had another five minutes, so she didn't open her eyes. The thought that she might reach over and turn the alarm off altogether flitted through her mind. Sleep had been elusive at best; she had been haunted by that damnable dream and memory of Anton's all-too-real kiss.

The alarm went off again. Dani started to stretch, felt a weight on her left foot, and stopped. Frowning, she sat up, wondering if her foot was merely asleep. She looked toward the end of the bed and nearly screamed, clamping a hand over her mouth in time to prevent her screech from escaping her lips. As if sensing she was awake, the black mass stirred. Suddenly four long legs stretched outward, and Dani found it nearly impossible to pull her gaze from the wickedly sharp looking claws that came into view. Her stomach churned. Pichouette's mouth opened in a wide yawn, displaying long, deadly looking white fangs.

Dani swallowed hard. "Nice cat," she said softly. "Now get off."

Pichouette turned and stared at her, the animal's green eyes changing to a deep impenetrable emerald by the soft light that filtered in through the open curtains on the French doors. She stood and stretched again, flicking her tail in the air, then gingerly walked toward Dani, her paws sinking into the coverlet with each step.

Dani cringed, remembering that long-ago feeling of claws raking across her temple.

Pichouette sat down next to Dani and merely stared at her.

Dani stared back. "Go away," she said hoarsely. "Find Anton. Find a mouse."

The cat cocked its head to one side.

Dani flicked a hand toward the side of the bed in a shooing motion. "Get down. Shoo. Go. Off the bed."

Pichouette leaned her head over and rubbed it against Dani's arm.

Dani jumped and nearly screamed.

Pichouette rubbed some more, then stopped and looked up at her. The cat meowed, then began to purr.

"Go away," Dani said, though not quite as harshly this time.

Pichouette moved closer and rubbed Dani's arm again.

Dani tentatively reached over and lightly scratched Pichouette between her ears, hoping she'd be satisfied and leave.

The cat purred and rolled over onto her back.

Dani stared at the animal's belly. Pichouette wiggled closer, gently touching Dani's hand with her paw. A sudden wave of compassion swept through Dani as she looked down at the huge black cat. "You miss your owner, don't you, Pichouette? You miss Sherry."

The cat's ears twitched, as if recognizing the name. She snuggled closer to Dani.

A knock on the door sent the cat skittering from the bed, and Dani nearly jumped for the ceiling. Another knock sounded, and the door swung open. Sanitee stepped into the room. "Good morning. I brought you some coffee, Miss Lane." She glared at Pichouette, who walked toward her. "What are you doing in here, lazy cat?"

"Oh, she's all right," Dani said, surprising herself. "I think we're friends now. Kind of." She smiled at the housekeeper, remembering the ludicrous thought she'd had the day before that the woman and the cat were one and the same. She'd obviously seen too many horror movies.

Sanitee looked sharply at Dani who was still sitting on the bed. "I thought you were afraid of the cat."

"Oh, I was." Dani smiled, then chuckled lightly. "But Pichouette has assured me I don't have to be frightened of her anymore."

Sanitee set the coffee tray down on the dressing table and turned back toward the door. She looked down at the cat again before leaving, then glanced over her shoulder at Dani. "Sometimes she lies," Sanitee said, and closed the door behind her before Dani could respond.

Dani spent most of the morning trying to avoid meeting Anton's gaze. Every time he called her into his office, she found somewhere to look other than at him.

Each time they were together she kept reminding herself that she was at Bayou Noir because of her job, not to have an affair. He was a story to her, a story that could catapult her career skyward. That's all he meant to her, nothing more. It was imperative that she remember that, keep that fact uppermost in her mind, and forget about how his touch had turned her body hot with a burning need that had throbbed within her all night long. She didn't want to think about what had happened between them, what it had felt like to be kissed by him, held by him. And she certainly didn't want to think about the stark longing and cold, bleak loneliness she'd seen in his eyes before he'd kissed her.

He was the means to an end. But the heat that rose to her cheeks, the tingling sensation that pricked at her lips whenever she remembered their kisses, kept calling her a liar and fed the guilt she was beginning to feel at her deception.

"Dani, fax this to Carter for me, would you please?" Anton said, breaking into her thoughts.

She waited for him to sign the document he wanted faxed, her gaze traveling over the other papers on his desk and stopping at one full of figures, several of which were circled in red. She darted a look at the top of the page and saw that its heading was "The River Queen." Her heart skipped a beat. The casino. She frowned and zeroed in on one figure that was circled in red, glanced at those jotted both above and below it, and then at the description for them in the left margin.

Her gaze moved to yet another, and repeated the same process, committing them to memory. She assumed something was wrong, otherwise why had Anton circled them?

He looked up and caught her gaze on the sheet of figures. A coldness came into his eyes that hadn't been there moments before. "After you fax this you can leave for lunch, Miss Lane. I'll be going in a few minutes."

Dani nodded, noting he'd addressed her formally again and knew he'd become angered at catching her trying to read his papers. She walked to the fax machine. Behind her she heard him gather the papers that were on his desk and slide them into a drawer, which he then locked. He moved past her to the door. "I'll be back at one."

She watched him leave and suddenly felt about two inches tall. He hadn't said anything, but by locking his desk he might as well have shouted that he didn't trust her. A deriding smile curled her lips at the thought. Trust her? She had no reason to expect that from him. The thought alone was preposterous. Even though he didn't know the real reason she was at Bayou Noir, he had caught her going through his files in the dead of night, he had caught her trying to read the papers on his desk while he wasn't looking. And she still couldn't figure out why he hadn't fired her that first night.

Dani closed up her own office and went upstairs. Once in her room she pulled out her cellular phone and dialed Stan.

"Yeah?" he growled into the phone.

She smiled. "Have you ever thought of trying a more pleasant way of answering the phone?"

"I knew it was you."

"Oh, right." She laughed. "Anyway, listen, I might have something." She rattled off the figures and names of companies she'd seen on the paper. "They were circled in red, so I assume something's wrong with them."

She heard the click of computer keys. "I'll say something's wrong with them," Stan barked into the other end of the line a few seconds later. "Those companies went out of business a while back."

"Out of business?" Dani repeated dumbly. "But then how could Reichard be using them to build the casino?"

"He can't," Stan said. "But he could be making it look like he is so he can skim money off the bank loan he and his partners took out for the venture."

Dani shook her head. "I don't think so, Stan."

"Then maybe someone else is, and Reichard caught them at it."

Somehow she knew, instantly, that was what was happening. "I'll call you back." She flicked off the cellular phone and changed clothes. Maybe she could still catch Anton before he left the stable. There were a few questions she wanted to ask him, subtly of course, and if she was lucky, he'd answer them . . . hopefully the way she wanted him to.

She saw the groom brushing down one of the horses in front of the stable area as she approached. "Hi," she called out. "Is Anton around?"

"He just left." The groom bent to rub a brush over the animal's stomach.

Dani paused beside him. "Think I can catch him?" she asked lightly.

The man straightened and looked at her. "Maybe. You want me to saddle Lady Jane for you?"

She smiled. "I'd appreciate it."

Five minutes later he helped Dani mount the gray mare.

"Which way did Anton go?"

He pointed. "Same direction you two took yester-day."

"Thanks." She nudged Lady Jane's ribs, and the mare broke into an easy lope. Within seconds they'd crossed the wide meadow beside the stable and moved into the shadows of the large oaks that bordered it. After only ten minutes of riding, Dani knew she was lost. How it had happened so fast, how everything had come to look the same, she had no idea. All she knew was that she had no concept which way was "back," and no clue where Anton was. Birds chirped in the trees, a cicada chimed in every once in a while, and small creatures scurried about here and there under cover of the tall grass that grew everywhere. At least she hoped they were small creatures.

She rode on, but moments later the silence was broken by the abrupt roar of a gator in the distance. The sound instilled her blood with a chill that shook her from head to toe, but since Lady Jane didn't spook, Dani decided she wasn't going to either. She reined up in the center of a clearing that looked identical to the one she and Anton had rested in the day before. Rested and kissed, her conscience reminded her. The memory drifted into her mind and brought forth a traitorous surge of warmth that washed through her entire body.

A sharp cracking sound shattered the air. A millisecond later something whizzed past Dani, so close that she felt the breeze it left slap her cheek.

Lady Jane reared, whinnying loudly and pawing at the air with her front hooves.

Someone had taken a shot at them. No sooner had the thought flashed into realization than Dani's heart nearly stopped beating as another report rent the air, and the bullet slammed into the trunk of a nearby tree. The horse screamed again. Dani clung to the saddle horn and gripped Lady Jane with her legs, struggling not to be thrown to the ground. Lady Jane's front legs slammed back to earth, and the mare bolted forward in a full-out gallop. Dani's hands dug into the saddle horn, and she leaned forward, her face only inches from the horse's neck. She made no attempt to guide the animal in any direction, knowing that in spite of her panic Lady Jane would instinctively make for home, and that was fine with Dani because that's exactly where she wanted to go.

Within minutes horse and rider broke from the bayou's overgrowth and crossed the wide meadow beside the stable. Dani saw the groom standing in the foal corral with a young horse, the lead rope having gone slack in his hand as he watched her mad-dash return.

Lady Jane skidded to a stop in front of the stable. Dani, legs shaking, fingers stiff, sore, and white, was still struggling to dismount when the groom ran up to her.

"What happened?"

She slid to the ground, thankful for his helping hand, and bent over, trying to get her breath back and slow the frantic beat of her heart. "I . . . I'm not sure," she gasped between gulps of air. "I think . . . someone . . . shot at me." The words had just left her mouth when, out of the corner of her eye, she saw the rifle leaning up against the stable wall, right next to the gate that led into the foal corral where the groom had been. She straightened and met the man's eyes.

"Sa c'est de la couyonade."

"It is not foolishness," Dani snapped, realizing at the slight widening of the man's eyes that he hadn't thought she'd understand the caustic Cajun remark. "Someone shot at me. Twice." She inhaled deeply, anger replacing fear now. "And if you don't believe me, I'm sure we can go back and dig the bullet out of the tree trunk it hit." *Except I'd probably never be able to find that tree or that clearing again*, she thought to herself, hoping the man didn't decide to take her up on her challenge. Then she realized if he'd been the one who had shot at her, she'd invited him to accompany her back into the swamp to finish the job. Panic seized her heart.

But the groom merely shrugged, seemingly unaffected by her rebuff. "Probably poachers." He held on to Lady Jane's reins as the horse kept trying to jerk away from him. "We get them sometimes in the bayou."

"I wasn't that far into the bayou," Dani said, her tone sharp. "I was in a clearing, and I don't think Lady Jane and I could really be mistaken for a gator, or whatever else a poacher might be trying to poach. Do you?"

The man merely shrugged again. "Maybe you got some bad enemies you don't know about then, hey *chère*?"

"What?" Dani stared at him in disbelief.

He turned and led Lady Jane back into the stable, obviously wanting to end the conversation. "I'd better brush the Lady down. Don't want her getting sick, no."

Dani stared after him, then her gaze moved back to the rifle leaning against the wall. Someone had taken a couple of shots at her, and she'd bet money it hadn't been a poacher. She walked to the rifle and, bending down, put her nose close to the end of the barrel and inhaled deeply. The weapon didn't smell as if it had just been fired, but then she was no gun expert. She turned to look back in the direction she and Lady Jane had been. Who else was in that bayou? And why had they shot at her? Or had it been an accident? Simply poachers, like the groom had suggested.

Suddenly the same high-pitched sound she'd heard the night before blared across the silence, startling Dani and causing her to jump. She laughed shakily at herself. If she hadn't known better, she'd have sworn there was an elephant in the bayou. But that was ridiculous. This was Louisiana, not Africa. She turned to walk toward the house. "Elephants," she muttered to herself. "Right. Next I'll be seeing giraffes in my bathroom and gorillas jumping on my bed."

The sound came again, and Dani paused and looked back at the thicket of trees across the meadow. If that wasn't an elephant's trumpeting blare, then what in blazes was it?

Dani walked back into Anton's study and found Sanitee dusting the statuettes that sat here and there on the bookshelves behind his desk. Smiling, Dani made the excuse that she thought she'd left her reading glasses in there, laughed that obviously she hadn't, and went back out. So much for trying to sneak another peek at those figures. But with the housekeeper in the study, maybe she could search Anton's bedroom. Dani hurried upstairs.

The house was as quiet as a tomb. She shivered at the thought, then opened the door to Anton's bedroom and stepped inside. No sooner had she done that than she remembered the snake. Her eyes darted around frantically. Was he in here? She felt an army of goose bumps march over the back of her neck. "Clyde?" she whispered, then rolled her eyes at realizing she was calling out to a snake. When, after a few minutes, nothing moved, she decided to chance it. She walked over to the dresser and rummaged through its drawers. They held nothing but clothes. As did the armoire. The desk set against one wall had writing paper, pen and ink, and envelopes. That was all. No journals, no ledgers, not even an address book. A framed picture of Anton and his late sister sat on one corner of the desk, and as Dani stared at it she suddenly knew without knowing how that Sherry Reichard had been the most important woman in Anton's life.

Dani walked to the dressing table. A lemonwood jewelry box, its lid inlaid with swirls of carved cherrywood leaves, sat on one end. She opened it, and her gaze flitted over an array of cuff links, a few rings, a gold chain necklace, and a couple of watches, then paused upon a small black velvet box that sat in one corner. Shrugging aside an onslaught of guilt, she picked up the box and pushed open its lid. Dani gasped at the two rings that lay in a fold of red satin. The engagement ring held a huge solitaire diamond set amid thick, glittering threads of gold that looped and swirled their way around the precious stone. The wedding ring lay against it, a thinner swirl of gold that she knew, on the finger, would fit snugly against the other ring, making it appear as one. She had never seen anything so unique, or so beautiful.

He really had intended to marry Jessica Beausoil. The thought came to her mind unbidden, but even more unexpected was the jealousy she felt because of it. Replacing the lid on the tiny box, Dani left Anton's room and returned to her own. For the next two hours she paced the room and the gallery, watching for Anton's return and trying to stifle the unreasonable jealousy that wouldn't seem to go away. She was going to get into Anton's files that night. She couldn't put it off any longer. She'd get what she needed and get out of Bayou Noir and away from its dark owner. Then life would return to normal.

A short time later she saw him ride across the meadow toward the stable. Dani walked to her door and down the hallway. Maybe if she met him before he reached the house, they could walk together and she could try to get him to talk a little bit. She didn't want to think it was merely an excuse to be near him, because it wasn't. She needed information for her story. That was all. There was nothing between them, except maybe physical attraction, and as far as she was concerned, she could control that.

Dani thought she'd meet him on the path between the stable and the house, but she didn't. She was nearly at the stable when she finally saw him. Anton was talking to the groom, the horse he'd ridden standing beside him. But it was neither Anton nor the horse who drew Dani's attention. Instead, she stared at the rifle settled into the leather scabbard that was attached to Anton's saddle.

NINE

"You son of a bitch," Anton said with a snarl, glaring at the man who sat in one of the chairs opposite his desk. "What in the hell do you think you're trying to do?"

"I'm not *trying* to do anything, Tony," Jim Knight lashed back, "I'm doing it."

Anton recognized the need for revenge that glimmered in the man's eyes, and called himself a fool for never having seen it before. But then it wouldn't have been something he'd have wanted to see, because it would only have intensified his own feelings of guilt. If Jim Knight harbored a need for revenge, it was because Anton had put it there.

"You have to be stopped, Tony, before you ruin everyone," Jim continued, "and that's exactly what I intend to do: Stop you."

"You could hurt a lot of people by doing this," Anton snapped. "And you know it."

Jim shrugged. "As long as you're one of them, Tony, I frankly don't give a damn."

Anton shot up from the chair behind his desk. "You

don't know what you're doing, Jim, what you'll destroy." He looked down at the legal papers Jim had tossed onto his desk, picked them up, and crumbled them within his fist. "I won't let you do this, Jim."

An ugly smile pulled at Jim Knight's mouth. "It's already done, Tony. I signed the papers this morning. There isn't anything you can do about it."

Anton grabbed the phone, then slammed it back down onto its cradle. "Dani."

The rage in his voice shocked her. She pushed away from her desk, where she'd been listening to his every word anyway, and walked into his office.

"Call Carter and Floyd and tell them to get the hell out here. Now!"

"It's too late, Tony," Jim said.

Anton settled an icy gaze onto the man whom he had once considered his friend, and if things had turned out differently, would have also been his brother-in-law. Now he'd proven he was nothing more than an enemy. "It's never too late, Jim," he said, his words edged with a white-hot fury that intensified the cold gleam in his eyes. "Obviously that's a fact you don't acknowledge, which is why you usually fail."

Dani shivered at the rancor in Anton's tone.

"But not this time," Jim retorted. He stood abruptly. "This time it's your turn to lose, Tony." The sound of the door slamming behind him echoed through the house.

Anton spun around and walked out onto the gallery. Dani stood in the doorway to her office, watching him. Rage, hot, white, and lethal seemed to surround him, roil about him, pulse through every muscle, dance between the fists that had begun to continually open and close, permeate the very air that encircled him.

The following half hour seemed the most interminably long she'd ever endured, but when Carter walked into Anton's study, with Floyd practically on his heels, Dani felt the tension in the house increase rather than diminish.

"What's the matter?" they both said, nearly in unison.

She hurried to the open door that led into Anton's office from her own.

He had been pacing on the gallery ever since Jim Knight had left. Now he stopped, whirled to face the two attorneys, and strode back into the room, his face a portrait of pent-up rage. "What's the matter?" he mocked. "I'll tell you what the hell the matter is. That son of a . . ." He paused and inhaled deeply, trying to calm himself. "Jim Knight bought up five hundred thousand shares of Lexicon stock."

Carter frowned. "So?"

Dani silently thanked him for prodding Anton into explaining, because she had no idea what Lexicon was, or why he was upset that Jim had bought shares in it.

"So?" Anton thundered, losing any grip he'd had on the composure he had been struggling to regain. "In the past three years Jim has blown his money on one bad investment after another. He's got a reputation now, and the only reason it isn't hurting us in the casino venture is because I co-signed his investment for him. The only way he loses with us is if I pull the plug."

Carter shook his head. "I still don't understand."

Anton pinned him with a glare that would have wilted most men.

"Jason Verielle is president of Lexicon," Floyd Pellichet said. "Two years ago Jason and Jim Knight were best friends and Jason owned his own company. Then Knight talked him into investing everything he had into the Deveraux Fund."

"Remember the Deveraux Fund, Carter?" Anton said with a growl.

The blond attorney nodded, suddenly looking, Dani thought, a little sick.

"Then you remember that the Deveraux Fund went belly-up," Anton said, continuing. "Jason lost everything, including his company." Anton began to pace again. "If Jason quits Lexicon because of Jim's involvement with it, some of the major shareholders will undoubtedly panic and sell off their stock. If that happens, Lexicon could fold, and the principal I get from my shares in it, which you both know are substantial, will disappear." He stopped pacing and turned to stare at them. "It wouldn't break me, or even come close, but that money is what I use to fund my private interests." He slammed a fist down on his desk. "I don't want to lose it." Anton's blazing glower turned on Carter. "Is that clear enough for you, Carter?"

Both attorneys remained silent, knowing better than to ask what Anton's private interests were. They'd each made that mistake in the past, and for their trouble they'd received a thundering explanation of what the word *private* meant.

"What do you want us to do?" Floyd asked, drawing every eye to himself.

"You both have access to my accounts," Anton said. "Buy up every share of Lexicon you can get your hands on, and do it quickly, before word of this gets out. I want control of the company or, at the least, more control over it than Jim Knight has."

Both men nodded and turned toward the door.

"And find out where he got the money to buy the shares in the first place," Anton called after them, "because he didn't have it a few months ago when he begged me to let him invest in the casino venture."

The outer door closed, and quiet descended on the study again. Dani glanced at her watch. Five to four. Would he still go out with this crisis hanging over his head? She hoped so. It would give her time to get upstairs and phone Stan.

"Okay, Stan, did you find out anything?" Dani asked, not wasting time on cordialities when he answered his line.

"Yeah. Several of the companies you named that were on Reichard's list had been owned by a holding company, Sandcastle, Inc., out of Boston."

"And who owns that?"

"I'm still trying to find out. And we ran a check on that housekeeper, like you asked. She's clean. Carter Tyrene likes the ladies and spends a lot on them, lives a bit beyond his means most of the time, but we haven't come across anything illegal on him. Pellichet has a big mortgage on a house over on Lake Pontchartrain, and a condo down in the Keys, but that's it. Both seem okay."

"Well, one of them's not," Dani said. "Any more on Jim Knight?"

"Nothing illegal. He's kinda like Reichard. Ever since the accident the only thing he's done is pay attention to business. Doesn't see anyone, doesn't go out much, doesn't party. Only difference between the two is that Reichard seems to make money on his ventures and Knight loses it."

"Yeah, well he just did something that set off fireworks out here like the Fourth of July. Check on his finances again, Stan, and look deep. He bought five hundred thousand shares of stock in a company called Lexicon, and Reichard's furious."

"Call me back tonight," Stan ordered.

For a long time after they hung up, Dani thought about Stan's last words. *Reichard seems to make money—Knight loses it.*

He'd had a hundred things to do that afternoon, and uppermost was the problem with Jim and Lexicon, but Anton couldn't keep his mind on any of it. He rose from his desk and walked to the door that connected his office to Dani's. "I'll see you at dinner," he said brusquely, then turned and left the room before she had done little more than acknowledge his comment by looking up from the letters she was stuffing into envelopes.

The entire day had been torment, because through everything that had happened, including the confrontation with Jim Knight and the resulting problems concerning Lexicon, he hadn't been able to give those matters his full concentration the way he was used to doing. Instead, images of Dani Lane, memory of the way she'd kissed him the night before, kept invading his thoughts. He'd tried to concentrate on work that morning and had seen her face everywhere he'd looked. He had argued with Jim, and remembered the way her blue eyes had been filled with fear when she'd seen Clyde in her bed, and the way they'd become a mirror of the passion that burned within her when they'd kissed. He had met with Carter and Floyd, and even while ranting at them, he couldn't stop his mind from conjuring up images of Dani wrapped in nothing but a towel, and remembering how badly he'd wanted to run his hand along the creamy flesh of those long, lean, exposed legs.

But he'd wanted more than that. He had wanted to make love to her, and the acknowledgment of that desire, the memory of it, had been taunting him ever since the moment she'd pushed him away. It had taken every bit of his will to leave her that night and return to his own room instead of dragging her back into his arms to plunder her mouth with his.

He turned from the path leading to the stable and crossed the wide meadow beside it on foot. Normally he rode to the compound, but this afternoon he felt like walking. He needed peace and quiet, he needed time to think, he needed to burn off some of the emotions roiling through him, especially the ones he felt toward Dani Lane. The ones he didn't want to feel.

Anton strode through the bayou, paying no attention to which way he was going, but then, he didn't have to. He could find his way blindfolded if he had to. The route had become a habit, ingrained in his subconscious. Across the meadow, left at the clearing, right at the stream, past Catfish Jones's old cabin, straight through the copse of bayou foliage for a mile, then right at the cypress stump, left at the rotted hull of his grandfather's old pirogue, and there they were.

Twenty minutes later he passed the pirogue and after walking a few yards more, stopped at a tall wrought-iron gate. He pulled a key from his pocket, inserted it into the lock, and pushed the gate open, closing it behind him. He looked around slowly but there was no sign of them. Anton laughed softly. He knew they were there, behind the rubber plants, ferns, cypresses, and palmettos, waiting for him to call out.

Dani urged Lady Jane past the clearing. It was the same one in which she'd paused the day before while riding the horse. Someone had shot at her then. She hoped it wouldn't happen again, because this time they might not miss. She shivered as her mind replayed the entire scene, but she refused to give in to the terror the recollection brought with it. She turned her thoughts to the story. That was why she was there, that was all she should be thinking about. Stan had run into a dead end so far trying to find out who owned Sandcastle, Inc., and he hadn't come up with any other useful information. But now something else was going on, the thing with Lexicon and Jim Knight, and Dani suspected it and Anton's "private interests" might be a bigger story than the casino venture, if she could uncover exactly what they were.

A niggling feeling of guilt tugged at her senses, and she shrugged it away. She was a reporter, and if she didn't get this story, someone else would, then their career would go zooming upward instead of hers. Determination settled onto her shoulders. No one was going to get this story but Dani Coroneaux. "Come on, Lady Jane," she said, "Anton has to be around here somewhere."

Staring at the ground, Dani tried to make out where Anton had gone, but she was no Indian tracker, or any other kind, for that matter. "Left," she decided, and pulled the horse's reins in that direction. Five minutes later, with Lady Jane hock-deep in bayou water and a gator lying only a few yards away, one eye watching their every move as if he were trying to decide which would taste better, Dani or the horse, she decided they were going in the wrong direction. Though even if it was the right direction, she wanted to change it before the gator decided that it was time to act.

An hour later she had to admit to herself that she was lost, but she wasn't afraid this time because she knew that if she gave Lady Jane her lead, the horse would take them home. They came to a small clearing, and since the ankle she'd twisted when she'd panicked at Pichouette's little surprise lunge from the armoire had begun to ache, Dani decided to stop and stretch her legs. She slid from the saddle and, as her feet touched the ground, bent over, then straightened and raised her arms high above her head. She turned to rub a hand over Lady Jane's neck, and the animal suddenly whinnied and jerked to the side as if startled, then bolted toward the trees. Stunned, Dani stood and watched the horse run away, the inclination to scream out her name or lunge after the flying reins coming all too late.

She glanced at the watch on her wrist. Six. "Great," she muttered. The sun would be going down shortly, and she was heaven only knew where. A shudder of fear tripped across her shoulder blades, like fingers of ice that left her cold both inside and out. Dani tried to ignore the sensation, as well as the fear quickly building inside of her. Hysteria would get her nowhere.

"Neither will being brave," she snapped at herself. She looked up at the waning sun, wishing she'd done what her mother had wanted years ago and become a Girl Scout. At least then she might know in which direction to start walking.

Half an hour later dusk had fallen over the bayou, shrouding it in a contrasting tableau of light and shadows, and Dani's hysteria was quickly beginning to take firm root of her senses. Bushes rustled, waters rippled, and grasses swayed. Each time Dani heard even the slightest noise, or noticed even the slightest movement, she nearly jumped out of her skin, imagining what was lurking behind, beneath, or around whatever moved. A chorus of cicadas hummed, their calls filling the night and driving away the silence, though Dani wasn't certain she preferred hearing them to hearing whatever else might be out there, stalking her. When darkness finally crept over the entire landscape, Dani found herself on the verge of tears, ankle-deep in murky, black water, and shivering from both the cooling night air and the chilling fear that was threatening to pull her into a mindless chasm of panic.

"Keep going, Dani," she muttered. "Keep going and don't think." Something swished through the water at her feet. She looked down and froze in terror. Every organ in her body seemed to cease its toil, except for her heart. It slammed against her breast over and over in what sounded to her like deafening thuds. A water moccasin swam past, its long, dark body curving through the water gracefully. The moment the deadly snake was gone Dani wanted to run. But overgrown foliage surrounded her, and she didn't want to hazard even a guess as to what might be lurking within or beneath it. Spotting an old cypress stump sticking up out of the water a foot away, she moved toward it and crawled onto its jagged top, pulling her feet up and wrapping her arms around her knees. She began to rock back and forth and hum an old song that was one of her favorites. It was the only way she could keep the terror at bay and have any hope at all of hanging on to her sanity.

"What do you mean she hasn't come back?" Anton growled at the groom.

The man shrugged and wiped a large, gnarled hand across his bald pate. "She said she was going after you, so I figured she'd found you."

"You know better than that, Tom." Anton strode to the stable door, stared out into the darkness of the swamp, then turned and stalked back to the groom. "How long ago did Lady Jane return?"

"About an hour ago, maybe more."

"And you didn't think anything of her coming back riderless? That maybe there'd been an accident?"

"Like I said," the groom repeated, "I didn't notice the horse right away, and when I did I figured Miss Lane was probably walking back with you. Wasn't no marks or nothing on the Lady to make me think an accident or anything had happened."

"Saddle Starr," Anton ordered brusquely. "And get me a couple of flashlights and a blanket."

Five minutes later, after retrieving his jacket from the house and ordering Sanitee to put on a kettle for tea, open a bottle of whiskey, and warm up an electric blanket, Anton mounted the large black stallion and returned to the bayou. He rode for an hour, letting the thin beams of moonlight that managed to wangle their way between the swamp's growth guide him, while using the flashlight to peer into the darker depths where everything grew so close, so thick, that sometimes even sunlight didn't penetrate.

Then he heard her and reined in, sitting quietly in his saddle and somewhat startled, as he listened in disbelief. She was singing. He cocked his head, momentarily convinced that his mind was playing tricks on him.

"Three little kittens all in a row, one says yes and the others say no, three little kittens all in a row. . . ."

Anton shook his head in wonder and turned his horse toward her voice. Whoever Dani Lane really was, she was one of a kind.

Dani heard a thrashing sound in the bushes and stilled. For a terror-seized instant the connection between sanity and calmness disappeared. She stiffened, prepared to bolt away from whatever creature was about to break forth and attack her.

Anton brought his horse to a halt and looked around uncertainly when Dani stopped singing, not wanting to move in the wrong direction. "Dani?" His deep drawl echoed through the quiet bayou.

Relief, like a wash of weakness, swept over her, so intense in its assault, she nearly fell from the cypress stump.

"Dani, where are you? Talk to me."

"Here," she called, feeling the sudden urge to jump from the tree stump and splash through the water toward his voice. Only the impenetrable blackness and slight swishing sound in the water kept her still. "Here."

"Keep talking so I can follow your voice."

Dani struggled to maintain her balance on the stump. "I'm here, on a cypress stump, over here. Over here." Lord, she'd never been happier to hear another person's voice. "Over here," she called out again.

"What did you think you were doing, coming out here alone?" Anton yelled back, his worry now edged with anger at her foolhardiness.

"Just . . . just taking a ride," she lied. "I . . . thought it would be nice, and . . . I needed some air and . . ."

Something splashed into the water beside Dani, and she screamed.

"Dani?"

"I . . . I'm all right," she said. "Just a gator, or a snake or something. Oh, Lord," she wailed softly, "only a gator or a snake. I'm crazy. What am I doing out here?"

"That's what *I* just asked you," Anton snapped.

Starr's head broke through the thicket at Dani's left, and she nearly leapt off the stump in fear of the monstrous black shadow that suddenly rushed toward her from the foliage. Anton's face moved into a scant ray of moonlight a second later, and Dani sighed and fought the urge to propel herself into his arms.

Starr splashed through the black water and at a jerk on the reins from Anton, stopped beside her.

"Do you know what could have happened to you out here if I hadn't found you?" he growled.

"I don't want to know," Dani said.

"No, you probably don't." He fought to keep both his voice and the look on his face gruff, but the sight of her huddled on the stump, and the memory of the ditty she'd been singing to keep her spirits up, threatened to turn his scowl into a smile. He reached down and slipped an arm around her waist, pulling her up and into the cradle of his lap.

Dani clung to him, too awash with relief, gratitude, and a myriad of other emotions to utter a word.

"I had about given up hope of finding you tonight," Anton said, his tone suddenly softer, intimate.

She felt the warm strength of his arm wrapped around her waist, the solid muscle of his thighs beneath her legs, and reveled in the sudden safety his embrace offered, and the sensations that erupted within her body because of his nearness. Her flesh quilted with goose bumps as he shifted position in the saddle, deliciously warm, enticing, tantalizing goose bumps, the complete opposite of those she'd felt a short while earlier when she'd been half scared out of her mind.

The horse moved slowly through the moonlight-dappled bayou, each step he took causing Anton's body to move caressingly, seductively, against Dani's. Her awareness of him increased tenfold with each passing second. Every breath she took brought her the musky scent of the bayou. It permeated the air and clung to Anton, and beneath that scent was the fragrance of the man himself, a blend of masculinity and cologne that teased not only her nostrils, but her senses. His body moved against hers, taunting, provoking, intensifying her cognizance of the strength that was harbored within his muscular frame, and the soft waft of his breath as it moved lightly, rhythmically across her neck.

Her rescue was turning into a uniquely sensual ride, and she was beginning to feel grateful to Lady Jane for running off. She was being saved from the blackness of a primeval forest by a dark knight on a dark horse who was surrounded by dark mystery and thoughts, and she was more attracted to him than she had ever been to any man. The realization frightened her. Darkness had always been something she had tried to avoid in her life.

Anton found, all too soon, that having Dani settled in his lap and pressed tightly up against him stretched the restraints he held over his self-control to a point where he wasn't certain how much longer he could endure having her so close. Loneliness, emptiness, and yearning welled up inside of him, raw and potent, and he silently cursed himself, her, and the circumstances that had brought about this situation. He wanted her desperately, and he could no longer deny it. Within seconds, he knew, he would no longer be able to ignore it either.

As if sensing a sudden change in his master's mood, the huge black stallion paused in the center of the same clearing Anton had taken Dani to the day before. Now lit by soft moonlight and a thousand stars strewn across a sky that was as dark as ebony, as endless as forever, the clearing seemed an exotic oasis of serenity tucked within a forest of primitive beauty and danger.

Anton twisted slightly in the saddle, his movements precise but unconscious.

Dani turned to meet him, her heart hearing the silent beckoning of his, even if her mind did not.

His head lowered, and his lips took hers.

He knew his mouth was hard and hot on hers, his kiss a hungry assault driven by the fierce need that erupted within him at her nearness, and the concern that had driven him to find her in the bayou. He had punished himself for three years, and now he was barreling headlong into exactly what he had vowed never to experience again. His soul would rot in hell, and he knew with the morning's dawn would also come regret and a self-loathing more profound than he'd felt since the accident, but he could no longer deny himself what he wanted so badly. When he looked at Dani's face, felt her in his arms, wanting her was the only coherent thought left in his mind.

His kiss gentled, coveying an agony of need and loneliness he was surprised to find were returned in kind. In her kiss, in her heart and soul, Anton sensed a kindred spirit, and knew, no matter what happened now, he was lost to her.

She opened her mouth to his, and Anton's tongue slipped forward to dance a duel of sensuality with hers. His hand moved to her breast and slipped inside the blouse whose button had broken away earlier, when she'd tried to find her way out of the bayou and snagged the silky fabric on the stiff, dead limb of a dry bush.

The seductive drag of his fingers over her breast created sparks of need that flowed through her veins to pool, hot and seething, deep down inside of her. Dani knew she shouldn't respond to him, knew she should push him away. She was losing all perspective, all professional demeanor and ethics, and she didn't care. What she was doing was wrong. She was betraying Stan, betraying her career, even betraying herself, but it didn't matter. None of it mattered, not at this moment, and maybe never again. She needed Anton Reichard to love her. She needed his strength, his warmth, his power. She needed his arms around her, his lips crushing down upon hers, his body pressed close.

He was the type of man she had always avoided—dark, secretive, brooding. A loner. Attributes that should have made it easier for her to turn away from him, yet seemed to attract her to him all the more.

Without being aware of what was happening, Dani felt him rise slightly in the saddle. He took his mouth from hers, smiling at the soft moan of despair that whispered from her lips at the loss of his. Swinging one long leg over the horse's rear, Anton lowered himself to the ground, threw his jacket down onto the lush grass that grew in the clearing, then reached up for her.

She went to him willingly, eagerly, her tired muscles relaxing against his body as he pulled her close and waves of desire ripped through her.

His mouth instantly claimed hers, ravaging ruthlessly, his tongue insistent now, exploring deeply, seductively gentle yet fiercely demanding. Every last thought she had of resistance, every reservation that had filled her mind only moments before, flitted away like dried leaves upon a winter's breeze. Need, hot and searing, began to stir deep in the core of her, aching and hungry.

Without taking his mouth from hers, Anton's hands held her arms and silently beckoned her to follow him as he lowered himself to the ground until they were lying on the jacket he'd thrown down moments before. His hands moved over her body in a series of caresses that were so light, so tender, so teasingly erotic that Dani arched toward his touch, silently pleading for more. And each time he obliged she shivered with a pleasure so intense, it left her breathless.

"Dani," Anton whispered hoarsely, "I . . ."

She moved her lips to meet his, kissing him with a gentle violence that silenced his tongue and fired his desires. She didn't want to hear his words, afraid of what they might be. There was no future for them together, she knew that, and was not fool enough to try to convince herself otherwise, even now, when passion's aphrodisiac worked on her body and senses. For them there was only now. Anton had his ghosts to fight, and she had hers, and even if they could get past that, once he discovered who she really was, why she'd really come to Bayou Noir, he would hate her. And she knew she wouldn't blame him, because part of her, at this moment, hated herself. Later she might have to face his regret, and maybe even her own, but not now.

Dani felt his fingers brush aside the front of her blouse and release the small hook nestled between her breasts at the front of her bra. Then his hands were on her bare flesh. The onslaught of yearning that shook her body was almost more than she could bear. She shivered uncontrollably as wave after wave of delicious pleasure, longing, and need erupted from deep inside of her and swept through her as his fingers teased, kneaded, and flicked. When he pulled his lips from hers and moved to take her nipple into his mouth, she felt the blood in her veins still, then turn into a volcanic flow of fire that burned her from the inside out.

TEN

Tightness squeezed at Anton's chest. That she had lied to him, that she continued to lie to him, was at the moment of no consequence. He couldn't remember ever wanting a woman as much as he wanted Dani Lane now, having ever considered a woman as tantalizing, as beautiful, as she looked lying beside him. Her blue eyes, like sapphires that had stolen the stars from the night sky, pulled him to her, beckoning, teasing, promising, and he was helpless but to heed their call.

He could warn himself against her, but he knew it was too late for that. She was innocence and danger, truth and lies, temperance and temptation, wrapped into one, and maybe it was that very combination, that melding of total contradictions that tantalized him in a way he had never experienced before.

Her lips tasted like warm honey, promising and alluring, while her scent of lavender surrounded him. The fever of wanting her filled his mind and body, sweeping aside any reservations he'd had, vanquishing any thread of self-control that might still have been within his grasp . . . if he'd reached for it. The need within him for her was so desperate, so intense, that it astounded him. He had no will left but to have her.

Dani felt as if she had been captured by a thunderstorm, a deliciously hot summer thunderstorm that was exploding within her, catapulting feelings and sensations through her body that she'd never known she was capable of experiencing. They were consuming her, overwhelming her, drawing her into a maelstrom of need so fierce, it frightened her.

He touched her with tenderness, but she sensed the restrained violence within him, the anger and loneliness that were at constant war inside of him, battling for control and dominance.

His hands moved to her jeans and tugged them downward, over her hips and legs. The chill of the night air touched her skin, but as soon as it did, his caresses stirred her passion and warmed her blood. Her own hands roamed his chest, sensing, exploring, unbuttoning his shirt, whispering over the bared flesh that was so hard, so hot, her touches stirring his blood, heating her own. Her fingers paused at a slice of scar tissue upon his shoulder and, curious, she traced it lightly with the tip of one finger.

She felt him stiffen beneath her gently probing touch, as if about to pull away, and Dani suddenly realized, through the hazy intoxication of her passion, that it must be a scar from the accident. A scar on his flesh that represented a scar on his soul. On his heart. She forced her hand to move on, stroking and caressing, and felt him begin to relax again. Every nerve cell in her own body sizzled with anticipation and excitement, hungering to be touched, her own pleasures heightened by the sensual exploration of her fingers upon his flesh. His body was naturally hard and exercised to well-honed lines, his shoulders like mountains of granite contoured for strength and grace, his chest like a wall of marble carved to perfection by the masterful strokes of a sculptor.

For the second time in a matter of minutes, Anton pulled away from her.

Dani watched him take off his boots.

A slight rustling sound in the bushes at the edge of the clearing drew her attention and Dani frowned, momentarily afraid some creature was stalking them, about to pounce and make them its dinner.

Then Anton stood and shrugged out of his own jeans, and whatever was at the edge of the clearing was instantly forgotten. A gasp of pleasure caught in Dani's throat at the sight of the molded muscles of his thighs, the long, lean length of his legs, the prominent evidence of his need for her.

She raised her hands toward him, silently calling him back to her, offering everything she had to offer, asking for everything he wanted to give. Anton dropped to his knees and slid into her embrace. His body was hot next to hers, and felt right. The thought both surprised and comforted Dani. He kissed her again, a slow, gentle kiss that turned the ache inside of her unbearable. She pressed herself to him, needing to be closer, needing to feel his body touch every inch of hers. His hands moved artfully, masterfully, over her curves, a teasing touch here, a caressing flirtation there. A sequence of explosions erupted within her, sparks of need raced through her veins and a hunger to be one with him that was so strong, so all-engulfing, suddenly enslaved her.

The world could end at this moment, and she knew she wouldn't be aware of it. He filled her senses. He had become her reality. He had become her world. She loved him. She feared him. She needed him. But most of all, she wanted him.

He moved above her, settled atop her, his weight comfortable and welcome. She felt his arousal against her, teasing, touching the oversensitized and most intimate part of her body.

His lips moved on hers, his chest gently rubbed against her breasts, the fingers of his left hand curled within the tendrils of her hair as his hand brushed lightly along the curve of her shoulder, and the other hand moved to prepare her to accept him. Waves of pleasure washed over her like warm honey cascading over hot marble, melting her flesh, fusing it to his. She was drowning in a rapture that was beyond reason. His fingers moved inside of her, and she became wet and warm. Her need intensified, consuming her thoughts, controlling her actions. Her arms tightened around his neck, drawing him closer to her. Her tongue played with his, daring, begging, dueling.

The yearning to be one with him, to touch, taste, know every plane and curve of his body was a driving hunger that grew deeper, more pressing, more urgent, with each caress of his hands upon her flesh, each press of his lips to hers. She needed to feel his heat, his strength, his passion.

And then he entered her, and Dani knew that her world would never be the same.

He moved slowly at first, tentatively, as if afraid she would pull away from him, or push him aside. When she didn't, he probed deeper, his movements still tantalizingly slow, but surer. Her body enveloped him, her arms held him, her legs wrapped around him. The core of her drew him into her hungrily, and the craving, the yearning for him turned wild, ravenous, and uncontrollable.

She raised her body to meet his with each thrust. He filled her, she asked for more and he gave it, moving together to the rhythm of a song only their hearts and bodies could hear. Sensations that were both erotic and mind routing burst through Dani like a tempest, feral and unruly. She tightened her hold on him, crushing her body to his, deepening their kiss, pulling him to her with her legs, drawing him deeper inside of her.

His body enveloped hers, flesh to flesh, two becoming one, and Dani felt herself shatter into a thousand fragments of pleasure. Waves of warmth raced through every cell, every muscle, fiber, and bit of flesh. She shuddered from the force of her pleasure, and held on to him as he thrust into her one last time, their shared ecstasy rocking her senses and leaving her with no other reality than that of being held in the arms of a dark stranger who was truly no stranger at all. He was the man she had waited all of her life to find, the man she would spend all of her life loving. Yet even as the delicious, mellow glow of contentment settled over her, she knew he was also the one man she couldn't have.

He lay quiet atop her for several long minutes, his heart beating against her breast, his ragged breath teasing the side of her neck. The thought of moving away from her, of letting her slip from the circle of his arms was one Anton didn't even want to consider, and an event that although inevitable, he wanted to postpone for as long as possible. He nuzzled his lips against her neck, breathing deep of her scent and relishing the warm softness of her skin, which reminded him of the magnolia blossoms that grew in abundance around the plantation. "I've wanted to make love to you from the moment you came to Bayou Noir," he whispered, his voice deep and heavy with emotion.

The movement of his lips against her throat ignited a spark within every nerve ending in her body, and Dani shivered in delight. She snuggled deeper into his embrace. "And I've wanted you to," she said, not having realized the truth in her words until that very moment.

Anton brushed his lips across hers, pressed a kiss to each of her eyelids, then rolled off her and lay on his side, looking down at her. His body stirred with a renewed hunger that surprised him. He touched a hand to her cheek, then slid a finger along the curve of her jaw, down her neck to the hollow of her throat, across her chest. Then his touch, as light as a hummingbird's wing on an afternoon breeze, began making light circles around her breast, each just a bit smaller than the last, moving ever closer to her nipple.

Dani felt the hunger growing in her, the need to have him again, the yearning to touch his body.

His finger circled her nipple, then flicked at its hardened peak—once, twice, again and again—until she moaned aloud at the pleasure of his touch and the intensity of her newly aroused need.

Anton smiled, feeling a sense of happiness for the first time in almost three years.

Dani saw the smile and the hunger in his eyes, and reached out for him, pulling him roughly to her and taking his mouth.

If their first coming together had been a gentle demand, this was a feral conquering. Each took everything the other had to offer and gave back whatever was asked. His lips crushed hers, his tongue was a probing force that ignited flame wherever it touched, and his roaming hands savagely branded both her flesh and her soul as his. And with each demand he made, Dani answered in kind, satin lips drawing him into the fiery flame of her need of him, her own hands moving hungrily over the steely contours and granitelike hardness of his length and leaving an aching need everywhere she touched.

They moved together, each knowing what they wanted and needed. She took, he gave, she demanded, he surrendered. They reversed roles again and again, until finally Dani cried out, and he pushed into her with a shuddering tremor that left him weak and struggling for air but feeling more like a man, more like a living, breathing human being, than he had in a very long time.

He sank against her, trembling with the aftershock of release, his labored breathing gradually returning to normal, his body slowly cooling beneath the touch of the night air. Anton felt her stir beneath him and, thinking his weight was hurting her, he moved to lie beside her.

Dani stared up at the star-dotted sky and felt suddenly all too vulnerable lying naked beside this man who had just made the most glorious, wonderful love to her she'd ever known, but who for all practical purposes still remained a stranger to her. Feeling as if her body were on fire not from passion, but from the heat of embarrassment, she turned to reach for her clothes, dragging them toward her.

Anton's hand on her shoulder stopped her. "Don't," he said softly.

She turned to look at him, not certain what he

meant, but halted by the suggestion of supplication she heard in his voice.

"Don't run from me now, Dani."

She couldn't read his eyes in the pale moonlight that glowed down upon them, but the fragility of his words tore at her heart and deepened the sense of guilt that assailed her. Dani shuddered at the realization of the depth to which she had just betrayed everything she believed in. At the depth to which she had betrayed him. She averted her gaze, unable to look into his eyes any longer.

No matter how she berated herself for what she'd done, she knew she would cherish forever the moments she'd had with him. When he found out the truth about her, he would end up hating her. That, she believed, was inevitable now. She shivered at the mere thought of the confrontation between them that was certain to come.

Anton suddenly pushed himself up. "I'm sorry," he said, and held out a hand to her.

Dani started, her mind jerked back to the moment. She stared up at him blankly, not understanding why he'd apologized.

Anton smiled. "You're cold and you're right, we should go." A laugh slipped from his lips, and Dani realized it was the first real, happy-sounding one she'd heard from him. "I guess if we don't get back to the house pretty soon, Sanitee will send a search party out looking for us."

Dani nodded and reached for her clothes. At that moment, if she could have changed anything in the world, it would be that they never had to leave the one they had created together.

━━━◆━━━◆━━━

Sanitee let the screen door slam shut behind her as she hurried into the kitchen. "I knew she was trouble," the housekeeper muttered, and dragged off the galoshes that were half covered with swamp mud. She tossed them in the pantry and, retrieving several carrots and potatoes, began to peel them over the sink, her movements sharp and abrupt, fueled and tinged by anger and frustration. "I should never have let Carter hire her." She cut the vegetables into pieces and threw them into a steamer that sat on the stove, then bent to check the chicken she was baking in the oven.

The phone rang. Startled, Sanitee lost her grip on the oven door, and it snapped closed with a bang. She straightened and, glaring at the ringing instrument attached to the wall, wiped her hands on her apron and stalked toward the phone. If it was Carter, she'd give him a piece of her mind he'd never forget.

"Sandcastle, Inc., is owned by another holding company, which is also owned by another holding company," Stan said. "Which means the list could go on forever. This could take a while, Dani."

She nodded, but her mind wasn't really on the story. Instead she kept envisioning what was going to happen when Anton found out who and what she really was. Her stomach churned and her head throbbed just contemplating it. But worse than that, it caused an ache in her heart she knew would probably never go away. During the short ride back to the house she'd felt guilt, remorse, and regret settle onto her shoulders like a ten-ton weight. She'd fallen in love with him, and there was no future in sight for them that she could see but that he would end up hating her.

"Dani, dammit, are you listening to me?" Stan snapped.

She jerked from her reverie. "Uh, yes, right."

"As I was saying, Jim Knight got the money to buy those shares of Lexicon from some stocks he owned in a Brazilian company that had been having trouble and suddenly found the light, so to speak."

"All on the up-and-up?" Dani asked, frowning.

"Well let's put it this way, a few weeks ago those stocks were just about worthless, and our people haven't come up with any real reason why that status suddenly changed."

"Maybe Knight's in this with someone else. Maybe this business with Lexicon is an attempt to sabotage the casino venture?"

"How?" Stan demanded.

"Anton's been worrying over some numbers on the casino contractors. Mostly those Sandcastle ones, I think. Maybe this is an attempt to divert his attention from that." She frowned again as her suspicions took another giant leap on speculation. "Stan, is Jim Knight connected to Sandcastle? Or any of the companies that Sandcastle owned?"

"Not that I've found out. Why? What are you thinking?"

"I don't know. I'll check with you tomorrow."

It was almost time for dinner and she still hadn't dressed, but since she felt as if her stomach had tied itself into knots, she didn't think she'd be eating much anyway. She walked to the armoire and tried to decide what to wear, wanting to look especially nice, and knowing she shouldn't want that at all. The feeling that she was living on borrowed time, walking toward the gallows with the guillotine sharpened and ready to fall any moment, assailed her. "And it will be my neck on the block when he finds out the truth about me," Dani muttered. "No matter what else happens." She picked a blue crepe dress that seemed innocent enough with its long sleeves, high neck, and flared skirt, but its flattering lines clung to her figure and its color deepened the blue of her eyes.

After slipping into the dress, Dani returned to the armoire and reached onto its shelf for her black heels. She felt hair brush against her thumb and smiled. "Come on out, Pichouette, you little tease," she said, and laughed, amazed at how quickly her fear of the large cat had subsided once the animal had made the gesture of friendship toward her. She pulled the shoes from the closet, fully expecting the cat to leap out after them. Instead she looked down, screamed, dropped the shoes, and tore across the room.

Anton was running down the hall toward her as she flung the door open.

"What's wrong?" he demanded, grabbing her by the arms so tightly, she winced. "Dani, for God's sake, answer me," he growled, and shook her when she merely stared up at him, fear clogging her throat.

Dani broke free of his grasp and, whirling around, pointed at the large tarantula slowly crawling across the floor and away from her shoes.

Anton frowned and walked into the room, stopping only inches from the spider and crouching down beside it. "I don't believe this," he said, and put his hand on the floor in front of the creature.

"No," Dani screamed, terrified.

He glanced over his shoulder at her, but didn't move his hand. "It's all right," he said.

The tarantula paused at feeling his finger in its path, reached out one long, hairy leg to touch his flesh, then seemingly satisfied that everything was all right again, proceeded to crawl onto Anton's hand.

Dani shuddered.

Anton stood and walked toward her.

"Keep that thing away from me," she yelled, backing into the hall until she was hugging the wall.

"Isabelle is a timid soul who wouldn't hurt a fly, Dani, let alone you."

Dani stared at the spider. It was missing three legs and the thing kind of wobbled when it moved, but that didn't make her feel any friendlier toward it than she had moments earlier. "Isabelle?" she echoed.

He nodded. "I'll meet you downstairs."

Dani watched Anton walk down the hall toward his room, the large spider still cradled in the palm of his hand. She reentered her room and retrieved her shoes, wondering what else was going to jump, crawl, or slither out at her. A screeching peacock, a crippled snake, a deformed tarantula, and an unearthly blare that cut through the night and sounded a lot like an elephant, but Dani knew that was impossible. But then, considering what she'd already seen, why couldn't it be an elephant?

"Because elephants don't live in Louisiana," she snapped at herself. She looked back at the empty hallway. "But then neither do tarantulas."

ELEVEN

Anton stared at Isabelle as he dropped her gently into a shoebox after poking several airholes into its cardboard sides. "How did you get into the house, Issy?" he murmured. His mind had replayed every possibility, no matter how remote, and discarded each as improbable. Even if he hadn't distinctly remembered setting her back into her terrarium earlier, it would have taken her a month of Sundays to walk through the bayou, and if she'd somehow clung to his clothes, he'd surely have discovered her when he'd taken them off in the clearing.

The thought of taking off his clothes brought with it the memory of exactly why he'd done that, and an image of Dani's body pressed to his, hot and naked, brought a smile to his face he knew shouldn't be there. But he couldn't help it. She'd awakened something in him he'd never thought to feel again, something he'd vowed never to allow himself to feel again. And yet it was different from anything he'd ever felt before, stronger, deeper, and he couldn't deny it. Regardless of the fact that he'd only known her for a couple of days, and that she'd lied to him when she was around, when he thought about her the horror of the past didn't seem to hurt so much, and the future didn't look as bleak as it had before she'd come into his life.

Just thinking of her now turned his body hard and hot with want. His gaze and thoughts were drawn back to Isabelle as she stuck one long, hairy leg through an airhole, as if waving to him. Anton frowned. There was only one way the tarantula could have gotten into the house, and it was the same way he suspected Clyde had gotten in. Someone had purposely brought them there, and the reason seemed obvious: To scare Dani, and quite possibly make her want to leave Bayou Noir. The question was who? Who wanted to scare Dani? Who wanted her away from Bayou Noir? And why?

He thought about the fact that she'd lied to him about attending USL and wondered if she had lied about anything else on her résumé. Or maybe it was what hadn't been on the résumé that he should be concerned with. Whichever, he wondered now if it had anything to do with what was happening. As soon as the thought entered his mind, he discarded it. Whatever was going on, he knew, somehow, that it involved him, and he didn't have anything to do with Dani's past. Which meant it was more than likely that someone wanted her away from him.

Anton set the box containing Isabelle on his dresser. "I'll take you home later," he murmured to the spider, then turned and strode to the door. He went downstairs, but before going to the dining room he stopped in his study, picked up the phone, and punched out Beau Hammond's home number. A recording came on. Anton cursed silently and waited for the beep. When it came, he talked quickly. "Beau, this is Anton. I haven't heard back from you on those numbers. Call me. It's important. And while you're checking numbers for me, do a preliminary check on Carter's and Floyd's financial status."

Anton hung up and stared past the window and into the night, seeing the dark-shrouded garden with his eyes while his mind was elsewhere. He knew what he had to do. He'd been distracted for the past two days, but now he had to refocus on business. A cold hardness settled over him like an invisible cloak being draped over his shoulders. Something was going on, and whether it involved Dani Lane or not, he had to find out what it was before it was too late. There were too many loose ends appearing, too many surprises.

A long sigh of frustration rumbled from his lips. He didn't want to think she had anything to do with the problems concerning the casino, Lexicon, and the person who was betraying him, but he couldn't discount it. Not when he knew she had already lied to him. It was evident what he had to do now, but after what had happened this afternoon between them, he wasn't looking forward to it. Too many people, however, as well as *the others* could be hurt, even destroyed, if he let his personal feelings cloud his judgment. Closing and locking the study door behind him, Anton crossed the foyer and entered the dining room. He paused at the doorway when he caught sight of Dani standing in front of the French doors that led outside to the gallery. She was bathed in a caress of moonlight, the red-gold highlights of her hair having turned to a tangle of flaming curls, the pale blue dress she wore to an ethereal veil that draped her body in the most tantalizing manner. A hot coil of desire lashed at his insides, twisting into a knot that nearly caused him to groan aloud.

Sensing his presence, Dani turned from the window. Her eyes met his, and in spite of the guilt that was eating away at her, she smiled. She had been standing there for almost half an hour, and she'd made her decision. In truth, she'd made it earlier, while talking on the phone with Stan, though he hadn't given her a chance to tell him. She would though, the next time they talked. But it wasn't going to be easy to give up all of her dreams, and she had no doubt that's exactly what the course she'd decided to take would mean. "Is . . ." She shuddered just thinking of the monstrous spider who had been in her room. Dani tried again. "Is . . . what was her name . . . Isabelle . . . all right?"

"Fine." His voice was low and ragged from the emotion churning through him. He moved toward the table, motioning for her to join him. Anton waited until she'd settled into the chair at his right, then he took the one at the head of the table. He saw a movement in the blackness beyond the gallery, but the glass of the French doors, reflecting the light and interior of the room, made discerning exactly what he'd seen, or thought he'd seen, impossible.

Dani subtly took a deep breath, trying to calm the careening rush of her pulse the moment he'd walked into the room. "Is she your pet?"

He looked back at her, confusion clouding his blue eyes. Someone was watching them from the garden. He could only make out their silhouette within the dark shadows, but that was enough to know he was right.

"The spider," Dani said, dragging Anton's attention back to her. "I assume she's a pet?"

"Oh." He shrugged. "No, Issy merely lives on the plantation." He glanced toward the French doors again, but whoever had been watching them seemed to have disappeared.

Dani nodded as if she understood what he'd said, when in reality she was totally confused. The spider lived on the plantation, had a name, seemed friendly enough to Anton, but wasn't a pet. Which she assumed meant that Clyde the snake wasn't a pet either. Or the peacock. Or that trumpeting whatever-it-was. But if they weren't pets, then what were they?

Sanitee brought their dinner in, moving so silently, Dani didn't even hear the woman enter the room. She jumped when Sanitee suddenly appeared beside her. Dani waited for her heart to resume a normal beat. If she hadn't been a modern, intelligent, sensible woman, she'd almost be willing to start believing in some of the fantastic rumors she'd heard about the Reichards' housekeeper's having some kind of supernatural powers. She did seem to appear and disappear sometimes as if by magic.

Dani turned her attention to Anton and thought she saw a hint of a smile tug at one corner of his mouth. She knew her next question would most likely wipe it from his face, but she didn't have a choice. "I heard you talking with Carter and Floyd about buying shares of Lexicon," she said, ignoring the little angel of conscience who was flitting about the back of her mind and zinging her with guilt pellets. "Does that have anything to do with your interest in the River Queen and the talk I heard before coming here that you were thinking of pulling out of the venture?"

The room abruptly disappeared as his gaze turned as

dark and turbulent as a midsummer's gale hitting placid ocean waters. "Just what, exactly, have you heard?" he said, the soft, steely tone of his voice suddenly seeming much more menacing than either the look in his eyes, or the way one dark brow arched skyward in mocking inquiry.

Dani stiffened and forced herself to go on. It was too late to turn back, even if she'd wanted to. She shrugged, trying to seem nonchalant. "Only what I said, that the project is having financial difficulties, and rumor has it that you're thinking of pulling out, which would mean a lot of people could end up going bankrupt."

Irritation pinched the corners of his mouth. "Is that why you're here, Dani? To find out if the rumor is true?" His eyes bored into hers relentlessly, refusing to allow her to look away.

"No," she said with deceptive calm. Butterflies began to batter her stomach at how close he'd come to the truth. "I'm here because you hired me." *And because I love you,* a little voice in the back of her mind whispered.

"Let's assume for the moment that I believe you." A wary smile curved his lips. "I have no intention of pulling out of my investment in the River Queen Casino. And my aim to buy more shares of Lexicon stock has nothing to do with the casino."

"But Jim Knight's purchase of shares in that company did make you angry?" she persisted.

A knock sounded on the entry door before he could answer. Anton looked toward the foyer, listening as Sanitee crossed it and opened the door. Seconds later, she appeared in the doorway to the dining room. "Mr. Harlen Coroneaux has arrived," Sanitee said to Anton.

Dani nearly choked on the swallow of wine that was

just making its way past her tongue to her throat. She turned to stare at the doorway, knowing that her worst nightmare was about to explode into reality.

A tall, thin man with rangy arms and legs, a barrel chest, dark blue eyes, and a bushel of gray hair that matched the swatch covering his upper lip, brushed around Sanitee and walked into the room.

Dani watched in horror as Anton rose and walked toward her father, his hand outstretched in welcome.

Harlen Coroneaux was dressed in a brown tweed suit, a Sherlock Holmes–style hat, and round gold glasses that were perched on a beak of a nose that was the dominant feature of an otherwise long, softly defined face.

"Mr. Coroneaux," Anton said. "Please, come in, we were just finishing." He indicated the chair opposite Dani and glanced at the housekeeper. "Sanitee, please bring Mr. Coroneaux a glass of wine."

Dani looked into her father's eyes and felt paralyzed. She was certain her heart had stopped, her breath was caught somewhere in her lungs, and the blood in her veins had ceased to move. In fact, the whole world had stopped. These two men just hadn't noticed.

"This is my assistant," Anton said, "Miss Danielle Lane. Dani, this is Mr. Harlen Coroneaux, of the *Baton Rouge Gazette.*"

Dani forced her lips to curve in what she hoped was a smile and not a grimace. Would he give her away?

"Miss Lane," Harlen said, moving around the table to where she sat. She thought she saw a twinkle of amusement in his eyes and steeled herself for the words that would reveal her deceit. Her father was relentless when he was after a story, and would destroy any reporter who got in his way if he had to. She had no doubt he wouldn't stop with her just because she was his daughter. He took her hand and, bending, pressed his lips to the back of her fingers. "A pleasure to meet you, my dear." He smiled. "A real pleasure."

Dani swallowed hard and pulled her hand from his, unable to believe her own ears. "Thank you." She turned back toward the table. What was he doing there? Why hadn't he given her away? And why was Anton being so friendly with him? She glanced in Anton's direction, but his eyes were downcast as he resettled himself into his seat. He didn't give interviews. Hadn't cooperated with the media in any way since the accident. So how had her father gotten an appointment to see him? And without even lying about who or what he was.

Harlen moved around the table and took the chair to Anton's left, opposite Dani. "I'd heard you had a new assistant, Anton," he said, "but I hadn't heard how pretty she was."

Dani flushed, but it wasn't embarrassment that heated her cheeks. She shot her father a nasty glare that she hoped told him to knock it off and leave.

He smiled and turned to Anton. "Now, about what we discussed on the phone this morning."

"Publicity for the River Queen Casino," Anton said, "without bringing me into it."

Harlen laughed. "Of course, if that's the way you want it."

"It is," Anton said.

So that was it, Dani thought. Anton assumed her father was there only to do a story about the new casino. She wanted to jump up and tell Anton, in no uncertain terms, that her father would never do a mild publicity-geared piece about anything. He loved scandal, notoriety, big stories about big people. She smiled sweetly and turned to her father. "Mr. Coroneaux, aren't you the reporter who did that exposé on the Landersons of Houma last year?"

To his credit, Harlen's smile did not falter. "Yes, my dear, I did," he said calmly. "Terrible tragedy, that. It pained me to have to write about it."

"More like a scandal than a tragedy, I thought," Dani said. She frowned. "And weren't you the one who uncovered that mess in the state capital a few years ago, with that senator? And his aide, wasn't it?"

"Yes, another disappointment in office, I'm afraid." His words were curt and clipped.

"Another scandal, I'd say," she offered, her tone so saccharine, she almost gagged. "You must get tired of always finding the unseemly side of things."

Ignoring her barb, he stared her down. "I believe the people have a right to know the truth about anything that affects them, *Miss Lane*."

She didn't miss his emphasis on her assumed name and knew it was a threat. If she didn't stop, he'd let Anton know, somehow, who and what she really was. Dani sighed. She'd have to go about this another way. "I suppose you're right, Mr. Coroneaux." She pushed away from the table. "But if you'll excuse me, I really am tired. I think I'll leave you two gentlemen to discuss whatever it is you want to discuss and go upstairs and read for a while." She smiled at Anton, who'd risen when she did. The urge to move into his arms, feel his body pressed to hers, his lips, his warmth, his strength, was almost overpowering. "Good night," she said breathlessly.

"Good night, Miss Lane."

She looked back at her father. "It was nice meeting you, Mr. Coroneaux. Perhaps we'll see each other again."

"Oh, yes, my dear, most likely over breakfast."

His smile was like that of a cat who'd cornered a mouse, and Dani felt a shiver of trepidation skitter up her back.

"Breakfast?" she echoed, suddenly feeling a need to clutch at the table for support.

"Yes. Anton's been gracious enough to ask me to stay, don't you know? So that I can get background information for my story, and he can approve its layout ahead of time."

Her legs almost buckled. Dani looked at the man she'd known all of her life, the man who had never paid more than dutiful attention to her, and whom she'd always tried to please, and suddenly wished she could shove him into an envelope and mail him to the next universe.

She barely made it up the stairs and to her room, her entire body trembling with a combination of fear and anger. Taking the cellular phone from her bag, she punched out Stan's home number and drummed her fingers on the nightstand while waiting for him to answer. "Go to the kitchen and help your mother, Dani, like a good girl," she mimicked, not knowing how many hundreds of times she'd heard that from her father. "No, you can't play ball with me and your brothers, Dani. Go help your mother with dinner. No, girls don't bowl, Dani. It's not ladylike. Why don't you help your mother with the house? Why don't you go shopping with your mother? Why don't you . . . Stan, it's me," she said, bouncing from the past to the present the moment she heard the other line being picked up.

"Jeez, Dan, you have rotten timing. I was just—"

"Harlen's here," she cut in, at the moment not caring in the least what Stan was about to do.

"Harlen? Your Harlen?"

The astonishment she heard in his voice matched what she'd felt when her father had walked into the dining room. "None other," Dani quipped.

"Holy . . . did he give you away?"

"No, and I'm not sure why. Have you heard anything? He's supposedly here to do a publicity piece for the casino, but I don't buy that. He does scandal, tragedy, and anything else that's anywhere near explosive, but he doesn't do fluff. And to him, publicity would be fluff."

"Yeah, I agree. But listen to this. Those dummy companies we were checking on that led to Sandcastle, Inc., and beyond . . . we finally got to the dead end and guess what?"

"I don't like guessing games, Stan," Dani snapped, in no mood to be nice.

"The whole thing was set up and owned by Floyd Pellichet."

"Floyd?" This situation was turning into one surprise after another, and if she didn't like guessing games, she liked surprises even less. "One of Anton's own attorneys is embezzling from him?"

"Looks that way," Stan said, "but we've got a little more digging to do before we can be sure Reichard's not behind this last holding company setup."

"I don't buy that, Stan, it's—"

"It's happened before," Stan said, cutting her off. "A

guy finds his finances going through the floor and decides to skim a little off the top to tuck away for himself when the bottom disappears and everybody else goes bankrupt. It's happened. I'll let you know what we find."

"What you'll find is Floyd Pellichet," Dani said.

TWELVE

The next day Dani felt as if the world had tilted on its axis and she was struggling to hang on. Anton was warm and courteous to her father, while brief and cool to her, and she had no idea why, unless her father had informed Anton about who she really was after all. But when the morning passed and Anton said nothing to indicate that, Dani knew his mood swing toward her had nothing to do with her father's appearance. Anton was being cool because he regretted what had happened between them. It was obviously that simple. They'd made love, and he wished they hadn't.

At three o'clock she was standing beside his desk, handing him some files and aching to feel the touch of his lips on hers, when his private line rang. He glanced at her, and she took that as a sign she should leave the room, but before she got to the door she heard him answer.

"Carter, what's wrong?"

Dani turned back and stared at him. He glanced up but didn't motion for her to leave.

"Floyd? What the hell happened?"

Dani felt Harlen move to stand behind her, listening to every word. She hesitated between the urge to remain in the doorway and listen herself, or step back into her office, forcing her father with her, and close the door so that he couldn't hear what Anton was saying.

Her own curiosity won out.

"Is everything taken care of?" He nodded. "All right. Keep me informed."

He hung up, and Dani walked back into the room. "Is something wrong?"

Anton looked up at her. His face had taken on a slightly ashen appearance, and there was an emptiness to his gaze she'd never seen before. "Floyd was in an accident."

She noticed the slight trembling of his hand. "Accident?" she echoed. "What happened? Is he all right?"

"Serious?" her father asked.

She glared over her shoulder at him. Go away, she tried to say with her eyes, but he just leaned against the doorjamb and ignored her, focusing his attention instead on Anton.

"Hit-and-run," Anton said.

"Oh, my Lord." Dani gasped.

"He was crossing Canal Street. A car shot around one of the trolleys, hit Floyd, and kept on going. No one got the license number."

"Is there anything I can do?" Dani offered.

"Arrange for flowers to be sent to the hospital," he said coldly, then reached for the phone, looking pointedly at Dani and Harlen.

"Is it serious?" she asked.

"He has a broken leg, a couple of cracked ribs, and a

possible concussion. Now, if you'll excuse me, I have some business calls to make."

Dani nodded and backed out of the room, forcing her father to heed her path. The emotional shield Anton had pulled around himself at hearing of Floyd's accident had been almost tangible. She closed Anton's door and walked around to sit behind her desk.

"Well, I've got to admit, you surprised me, Dani. I'll give you that," Harlen said.

She looked up at him. It was the first time they'd actually been alone together behind closed doors since her father's arrival. "What do you mean?" she asked warily.

He shrugged and laughed. "This," he said, motioning around the room. "We received a tip that a reporter had gotten to Reichard, but we didn't know how or who. I've got to admit, I never thought it was you. Took me totally by surprise when I walked in last night. Never would have guessed."

She glanced at the door to Anton's study, hoping he couldn't hear them, then saw by the light on her own phone that he was still talking on his, and looked back at her father. "Why, didn't you think I could do it?"

"Truthfully, no. But obviously I was wrong."

"As usual," Dani said, more deeply hurt by his comment than she cared to acknowledge. "At least where I'm concerned."

"Touché, my girl, touché." He moved to her desk and settled a hip on one of its corners. "Maybe I've been wrong about a lot of things where you're concerned."

She looked up at him, surprised, but not daring to hope. She'd been disappointed too many times.

"Maybe we can have us a little visit together when this is over, hey?" he said softly.

"Maybe," Dani answered.

He smiled. "So, what have you learned about this rumor that he's going to pull out of the casino venture?"

She stared up at him, unable to believe that he would expect her to tell him what she'd learned, even if he was her father.

He laughed. "So, not going to tell your old man, huh?"

"I was here first," she said curtly. "It's my story." Except that she didn't intend to do the story anymore. That's what she'd decided to tell Stan when she called him later. She had meant to tell him the night before, but then he'd hit her with the news that Floyd was behind Sandcastle, and she'd momentarily forgotten all about the fact that she had decided to quit the story. But it hadn't taken her long to remember. Even if it had, one look into Anton's eyes would have been all she'd needed as a reminder.

"We can both have the story," her father said, cutting into her thoughts. "After all, you write for the *Picayune* in New Orleans, and I'm writing up in Baton Rouge."

She shook her head. "There is no story, Dad," she said, praying she could bluff him into going away. "He's not pulling out of the casino venture, and he's confident he can outmaneuver Jim Knight's purchase of Lexicon stock."

"Lexicon stock?" Harlen echoed.

The moment he said the words, the instant she heard the surprise edging his tone, her head jerked up. Dani saw the look of interest that came into his eyes and knew she'd said too much. He hadn't known about Jim Knight and Lexicon. She wanted to bite her tongue off. Instead she shrugged, hoping the gesture appeared more nonchalant than she felt at the moment. "I told you, it doesn't matter." She smiled and rose. "In fact, I'm planning on calling my editor in a while to tell him I'm coming in. No point carrying this charade on any longer when there's no story."

"What about a story on Reichard?" her father probed. "The billionaire playboy who gave it all up and became a recluse? This decade's paradigm of the seventies' Howard Hughes."

"He's not as much a recluse as most people think," Dani countered. "To prove that, you're here."

Harlen frowned. "True, but it took a hell of a lot to get me in here. Believe me, more favors were pulled in and handed out to get this one than we've ever done before, and it still could be an interesting story, even if it is just on Reichard."

"No." She stared at him, willing him to go. With her palms flat on the top of her desk, Dani leaned toward him, her face suddenly hard. "He's had enough bad in his life, Dad, we don't have to add to it by robbing him of his privacy. And," she said, straightening, her tone suddenly sharp and threatening, "if you don't leave here too, I'll tell him why you're really here."

Harlen smiled. "I don't think so, Dani." He moved lazily around the room as if studying its decor, the books on the shelves, the chair beside the window, the lamp on her desk. Finally he stopped before her, a wily smile on his lips, triumph glittering in eyes the same shade as her own. "You're not going to tell him I want anything other than to do a publicity piece on the new casino, because then you'd have to confess to him who you are and why you really came here." The smile widened. "And since you've fallen in love with Mr. Reichard, I don't really believe you want to do that just now, do you?"

Her eyes widened in shock. "In love?" she repeated, trying to act as if what he'd said was the most preposterous thing she'd ever heard. Was she that transparent?

"Yes, my girl, in love." Harlen chuckled softly, as if reading her thoughts. "Or hadn't you figured it out yet?"

Dani stiffened at the derision she heard in his tone. "I don't believe in love at first sight," she snapped, "and I've only been here a couple of days. Long enough to know there's no story worth getting, but definitely not long enough to fall in love."

Harlen shook his head and looked at her.

She railed at the condescension she saw on his face. "I am not in love with him," she repeated.

He shrugged. "Believe what you will, Danielle, but I know what I know."

At that moment the intercom buzzed. Dani hastily picked up the receiver, noticing for the first time that her hands were shaking.

"Dani," Anton said, "I'm leaving early today. I'll see you at dinner. Tell Mr. Coroneaux, would you please?"

"Yes, certainly."

"And Dani?"

"Yes?"

"Don't go wandering into the bayou alone again."

He hung up before she could respond. *Don't go into the bayou alone again.* How else was she going to find out where he went every day at four o'clock? Dani looked back at her father and suddenly remembered that she didn't intend to do the story on Anton any longer, which meant she shouldn't care and didn't need to know where he went every day at four o'clock.

If anyone had told her several days earlier that she'd throw this story away, she'd have told them they were crazy. Her career had been the most important thing in her life for the past several years, and she'd finally gotten the job she had always wanted. She was a full-fledged investigative reporter with a major newspaper. It was all she'd ever wanted to be . . . until now. Now, suddenly, crazily, she didn't want that anymore, not the job, and not the story. So what difference did it make if she knew where Anton disappeared to every day?

Because you're dying of curiosity, a little voice in the back of her mind whispered. More importantly, she had a feeling that the only way she could protect Anton from her father was to find out what his secret was. Then she'd know how to steer Harlen away from it. Dani looked back at her father. "Anton's going out for a while. You're free to relax in the parlor until dinner if you'd like." She rummaged in one of her desk drawers, pulled out a file folder, and handed it to him. "This is a file on the casino venture. I'm sure you can come up with enough for your publicity piece by reading through it. You can also see by this file that everything with the project is fine, and going ahead. There's nothing there to make a scandal out of."

"And where will you be?" Harlen asked.

"In my room." She remembered suddenly how often in her childhood he'd told her to go to her room when she'd tried to interrupt or join in on whatever he was doing with her brothers. Dani smiled. Times had changed, and now going to her room and getting away from her father was exactly what she wanted to do. Breezing past him, she left her office and hurried upstairs. She'd intended to call Stan, but changed her mind. Pichouette lay curled in a ball on the bed. Dani saw the cat open one eye and look at her.

She smiled. "Just stay there," she said to the cat, "like a good girl." She wasn't really frightened of the cat any longer, but she couldn't help still being a bit leery of her. The memory of sharp nails raking across her face was a hard one to let go of, even though she felt certain Pichouette wasn't going to leap from the bed and attack her.

The cat stretched, pushing her long legs out in front of her, then curled back up and tucked her head into one arm.

Dani discarded the dress she'd been wearing and pulled on a pair of jeans and a T-shirt. Minutes later she was sneaking down the rear stairway and out the back door, hoping Anton hadn't gotten so far into the bayou already that she couldn't follow him. She ran down the path to the stable but there was no one around. A sense of disappointment rolled over her. She was too late, and the thought of going into the bayou alone, with her less than wonderful sense of direction, was not an inviting one. Dani turned to look at the thick copse of trees that bordered the meadow, and her spirits immediately soared. Anton was on foot. He had just disappeared into the shadows created by the wide-spreading and gnarled limbs of the massive oaks. She started off after him.

Farther back on the path between stable and house, Harlen stood and peered around the massive trunk of a tree and watched Dani follow Anton. "No story, huh?" he muttered to himself.

When she was halfway across the meadow, Harlen began to venture down the path after her, making certain to move slowly and stealthily, in case she glanced back. But he also made certain to keep close enough so as not to lose her.

Anton moved around the trunk of a large cypress and stopped, listening. He didn't hear anything, but he had the eerie feeling that someone else was in the swamp with him. His first thought was that it was poachers, but he shrugged that away. After he'd prosecuted the last one he'd caught, Carter had told him that word was out and others weren't going to chance trespassing on Bayou Noir again. A five-thousand-dollar fine and thirty days in jail weren't worth it.

Carter hadn't understood Anton's dogged determination to see the man he'd caught poaching on Bayou Noir prosecuted to the fullest extent of the law, and he'd said so more than once during the ordeal. But Anton hadn't cared if Carter or anyone else understood. They figured he was merely zealous about protecting the wildlife on Bayou Noir, and that was true. But he was even more zealous about protecting the others, because they couldn't protect themselves. They needed him. He needed them, and he'd do anything and everything he could to protect them. It was his memorial to his sister, to the secret dreams she'd once told him about.

He paused as an egret moved from the shadows to his right and took flight, a streak of white soaring through a single sphere of sunlight that cut through the thick treetops overhead. Anton smiled. Maybe it had been the egret he'd felt watching him. Humming softly, he made his way around several large rubber plants and the tall wrought-iron gate of the compound came into view.

Dani saw Anton stop suddenly. She darted behind a nearby tree and held her breath, afraid even the sound of her breathing would alert him to her presence and draw his gaze toward her. She glanced at her watch again, barely able to see the dark face and hands in the dusky shadows of the bayou. If she was right, they'd only been walking for fifteen minutes, long enough for her to get thoroughly lost and completely winded. Of course it hadn't helped any that she had to concentrate more on being stealthy than paying attention to where they were going. The last thing she wanted was for Anton to catch her spying on him.

The egret breaking from the shadows to her right nearly sent Dani scrambling up the tree. She closed her eyes and drew in a deep breath as her heart raced and her body sagged in relief. This had been a ridiculous idea, and if she had had any clue as to how to get back to the house, she'd have turned around and headed for it immediately. But she didn't, so she couldn't. She looked up, realizing enough time had elapsed that Anton must be ready to move on. Her gaze darted about frantically, and she nearly screamed in panic. He was gone!

Harlen cursed soundly beneath his breath and stared down at the three-hundred-dollar Loafers he'd purchased only the month before. Mud caked the sides of one and had completely covered the other, along with his sock, his foot, and halfway up his calf, when he'd slipped from a portion of the raised path and landed knee-deep in the water. His pant leg was dripping wet, his sock was down around his ankle, and he shivered just thinking of what kind of swamp creatures might have gotten on him in the two seconds his leg had been submerged. He looked for leeches and didn't see any, but wasn't reassured. He could only be thankful there weren't any snakes or alligators around. The thought sent a shiver of fear rattling through his body, and his gaze dashed back down toward the bayou waters. Nothing stirred.

He ran a muck-covered hand through his hair as relief took the place of fear within him, then cringed at realizing that he now had mud all over his head.

A bird shrieked from somewhere deeper in the bayou. Harlen jumped and jerked around, searching for the issuer of the sound and fully expecting some type of horrid swamp monster to come lunging out of the shadows at him. He'd lost sight of Dani a good five minutes before and had absolutely no idea where he was. Imaginary headlines flashed through his mind. *Pulitzer Prize–Winning Journalist Lost in Swamp.* He nearly groaned aloud. The only problem with that scenario was that he hadn't won the Pulitzer yet. "I'll get you for this, Grivere," he muttered, cursing his editor for giving in to Harlen's demands to do the story on Anton Reichard. When Harlen wanted to do a story, he was usually always given the go-ahead without much fuss, but this time, he was coming to realize, it might have been better if he hadn't gotten what he'd demanded.

He decided to turn around and try to find his way back to the house before Anton found him wandering around and helped him get back to Baton Rouge with a foot to Harlen's rear.

Dani heard something splash behind her and whirled around, staring into the gloom. For all the directional she had at the moment, Swamp Thing could come crashing through the bush toward her, and she wouldn't have the faintest idea which way to run for safety.

She turned and began walking in the direction she'd last seen Anton. "A gator," she told herself in an effort to bolster her courage. It was just a gator, probably splashing about in the water. The thought brought her to a complete standstill. A gator? *Just* a gator?

A shudder of dread ripped its way through her body and settled in a cold, coiled knot of fear in the pit of her stomach. Maybe she should call out for Anton. Dani took several more steps forward, moving around the tall rubber plants where she'd seen him pause moments before. She came to another abrupt halt. A set of tall wrought-iron gates stood on the opposite edge of a small clearing.

Dani frowned, totally puzzled, then walked hesitantly toward the gates. This had to be where he had gone, where he went every day, but what was it? Thin mesh wiring was attached to the iron rods of both the gate and the tall fence that branched off on either side of it. Glancing around and feeling like a thief in the night, she turned the gate's handle and gave a gentle push. It swung open silently. Dani stepped past the opening and closed the gate behind her, checking to make certain she hadn't locked herself in whatever it was she'd walked into. There seemed to be a path, not purposely carved from the swamp grass and foliage, but merely made by someone continually walking over the same ground, and it led into a copse of trees several yards away. Trying to ignore the trepidation tugging at every nerve cell in her body, Dani followed the path.

Just as she entered the copse, which was checkered by light and shadow, a dog trotted across her path, paused, and looked up at her in what she immediately recognized as a blend of fear and curiosity. Dani stared at the animal, not certain what was going on. He looked like a small poodle, and one of his rear legs seemed to be paralyzed. As if he'd satisfied his curiosity and was now ready to heed his fear, the dog barked at her, and then hurried away, dragging his useless leg behind him.

Dani didn't move. What was a dog, a crippled but otherwise healthy and seemingly very well-groomed dog, doing in the middle of the swamp and locked in a huge cage?

As if to confuse her further, she'd taken only a half dozen more steps when the most ferocious, intimidating roar tore the silence to shreds and her nerves right along with it. She knew exactly what that sounded like, knew it was impossible, and had absolutely no desire to prove herself wrong. With her heart in her throat she took three very hurried, very unsteady steps back, then suddenly wondered if the animal who had emitted that sound could be behind her. Terror seized every nerve in her body. She refused to look. If she didn't look, it wasn't there.

Dani nibbled on her bottom lip as her entire body trembled. It had sounded like a lion. A very big lion. But what would a lion be doing in the swamp? She remembered a movie she'd seen on television once where some quack scientist living in a jungle had conducted experiments turning people into animals. A chuckle that was more fear than humor slipped from her lips, and Dani shuddered. She was being stupid. And anyway, she hadn't seen any animal that even remotely resembled a person. Or vice versa.

And there was no lion. It was probably something else, some kind of bird or something. Didn't parrots imitate other animals? Or maybe it had been a recording, like those fake barking-dog alarms. She frowned and looked around hesitantly. But it had certainly sounded like a lion. "Now you're being ridiculous, Dani," she snapped at herself, trying to find some semblance of courage amid the fear streaking through her veins.

"Squawk! Now you're being ridiculous, Dani."

Dani nearly jumped out of her skin at the screeching echo of her words. "Who's there?" she demanded, her voice quaking.

"Squawk! Who's there?"

Dani swallowed hard and squinted in an effort to see farther into the shadows. A large red bird stood in the middle of the path a few feet away. It puffed up and, stretching its wings, flapped them. Dani noticed that one was much shorter than the other, as if part of it had been broken off. She frowned and took a tentative step forward. "Was that you making fun of me?" she ventured.

"Squawk! Making fun. Making fun," the bird repeated, then turned, flapped its wings again, and began to waddle down the path away from her.

Dani decided to follow, though she kept a close eye on each side of the path, as well as behind her and over her head. She hadn't forgotten the roar, and prayed it had been a recording . . . or a very gifted mynah bird.

She'd only recently conquered her fear of cats and made friends with Pichouette, though she knew that the edge of wariness she still felt around the cat meant she hadn't totally lost her fear of her. What she didn't need to undo that little progress was to come face-to-face with a cat who weighed several hundred pounds and had paws the size of her thighs.

No sooner had the thought crossed her mind than she followed the parrot around a curve in the path and froze, her heartbeat nearly coming to a complete and abrupt halt. "This isn't happening," Dani mumbled to herself, even as her gaze settled on the huge lion lying sprawled across the path, sunning himself in the warmth of the sunlight that had pierced the treetops.

It rolled to an upright position, shook its great mane, and turned to look at Dani. Swallowing hard as she met the gaze of those deep, unreadable brown eyes, she frantically tried to remember the words to a prayer . . . any prayer, but her mind was totally blank and seized by a terror she knew would most likely be the last thing she ever felt.

THIRTEEN

Dani watched the parrot waddle casually up to the lion. She held her breath, struggling to keep from turning in a panic and running as fast as she could back to the gate. Cat meat. She was going to end up being cat meat.

"Squawk! Freddy likes Boris. Freddy likes Boris."

Did lions eat parrots? Dani waited for the large cat to open its mouth and pounce on the colorful bird, then nearly laughed aloud with hysterical panic. Parrots? What did she care if lions ate parrots. Did lions really eat humans?

"Squawk! Squawk!" The parrot flapped its lopsided wings and hopped onto the lion's back.

Dani gasped, startled, and nearly jumped a foot. This was it. But rather than murderous mayhem, the lion merely pushed slowly to its feet, turned, and began to saunter down the path in the opposite direction from where Dani stood, the parrot riding jauntily atop the huge cat's back as if it were the most natural thing in the world to do.

"I've gone crazy," Dani muttered to herself. Her

hands were shaking, her heart slamming erratically, and her pulse was racing so fast, she wasn't sure why she hadn't fainted. "Crazy. That's the only explanation for all of this. I've just gone completely, utterly, one-hundred-percent crazy. Or maybe this is a dream." She pinched her arm, felt the pain, and knew, with a little sigh of despair, that she was totally awake. "Okay, I'm awake *and* certifiably crazy." She inhaled deeply, wishing she felt courageous instead of merely scared witless and stupidly stubborn. Peering cautiously into the shadows in search of the lion, she took several steps after it, wondering with each just what in blazes she thought she was doing following a lion. "I still don't even like cats," she grumbled, "so why am I following a lion?"

"Squawk! Freddy likes Boris."

Dani paused, a faint shriek escaping her lips. When her heart stopped smashing against the back of her throat, she forced her feet to carry her down the path again as she repeatedly told herself that if the lion had been dangerous, she'd already be dead and devoured.

Unless he wasn't hungry yet. "Oh, good, Dani," she snapped at herself. "Give yourself a little encouragement." The shadows of the bayou suddenly melted away as she came to a sun-drenched clearing. Anton was standing beside a row of small cages, his back to her. The lion sauntered up to his side.

Dani was about ready to scream a warning when the cat rubbed affectionately against Anton's leg.

"Squawk. Freddy likes Boris."

"Well, that's a real news flash," Anton said to the bird, and laughed.

The lion rubbed against Anton again, and he reached

down to run a hand through the cat's thick mane. "So, how're you doing, big guy? Ready to eat Freddy yet?"

In total awe, Dani stared at the clearing. Animals of every size, shape, and color were everywhere, lying, standing, sitting on the ground, on the branches of bushes, some perched upon fallen tree trunks or rocks. Rabbits, cats, dogs, squirrels, birds, possum, raccoons. And so many more, she couldn't identify them all. She saw Clyde curled on a rock, soaking up the warmth of the sun. Isabelle was perched atop a cage to Anton's right, and off to one side of the clearing stood a baby elephant, contentedly dipping its trunk into a small pile of peanuts and lifting them into his mouth.

A table beside Anton was half covered by an array of bottles, gauze, tape, and a variety of other things. Dani's gaze moved over the animals again, more slowly this time, studying them. Some had bandages, others did not, and though it wasn't apparent with every one of them, she knew, inexplicably, that each was injured or crippled in some way.

Her heart swelled with compassion and sudden understanding. This was where Anton came every day at four o'clock, to take care of creatures who could no longer take care of themselves. Tears filled her eyes. This was the world he'd retreated to since the accident that had taken his family from him. She had believed, like everyone else, that he had merely retreated to his home and into himself, but that wasn't true. He'd retreated here, to a world he could empathize with, a world whose creatures were just like him . . . injured and no longer able or willing to face the outside world.

She looked back at Anton and saw him smile at the parrot as he squawked again and flapped his lopsided wings. It was a genuine smile, only the second she'd seen from him since they'd met, and it touched her heart every bit as much as his lovemaking had.

"We all know you like Boris, Freddy," Anton said to the bird, "because he lets you ride him. Just stay on his good side, pal, so he doesn't decide to eat you instead."

"Squawk. Freddy likes Boris. Squawk. Now you're being ridiculous, Dani."

Dani felt the tension that suddenly descended on the clearing like a dark veil being pulled before the sun. She saw him frown, saw the way his shoulders stiffened and his hand, which had been gently stroking the raccoon who sat on the table before him, go still. "What did you say?" he asked the bird. Anton's smile had disappeared, his mouth tightening to a straight, hard line. "Say it again, Freddy. What did you say?"

"Squawk, squawk. Say it again, Freddy. What did you say? Squawk. Say it again, Freddy. Now you're being ridiculous, Dani. Squawk. Freddy likes Boris."

Anton swung around, and in spite of the distance that separated them, Dani saw the fury that blazed in his eyes and settled upon the rigidly held plateau of his shoulders. "What the hell are you doing here?" he demanded, his tone so austere and cold that she shivered from its icy touch.

She swallowed hard, her mind skittering about in search of an answer, an explanation, and finding none.

"What are you doing here?" he repeated, each word a thunderclap of barely controlled rage.

"I—"

He shook his head. "I should have known," he spat hatefully, cutting her off. His gaze bored into hers, mercilessly accusing. "Dammit, I should have known.

Sanitee warned me against you, but I wouldn't listen. Even Jessica knew, but I even shrugged aside my own suspicions because I didn't want to believe there was anything wrong, that you were anyone but who you said you were."

His words cut through her like a rapier slicing through tender flesh. All of her questions about the animals were momentarily swept to the back of her mind. Dani's stomach turned upside down, and a slight trembling assaulted her hands. "What . . . what do you mean? What did Sanitee . . . what did Jessica know?"

The smile that had been so sweet the second before, when he'd been talking to the animals, turned sardonic, tinged with rancor as he glared at her. "You aren't who you say you are, Dani. You didn't go to USL, and Carter hasn't been able to find any record that you've ever had a husband or a child." He chuckled softly, but the sound was not a warm or pleasing one. "But I wanted to give you the benefit of the doubt, so I didn't listen to my own misgivings when they told me to get rid of you. That you'd probably been sent here to spy on me."

"No," Dani said, even though she knew she was denying the truth.

"Sanitee warned me. She saw what was happening between us, and knew you weren't good for me." He shrugged. "But I wouldn't listen. That's always been my problem, you know? I've always done exactly what I damned well please, and hang the consequences." A rush of anger and sorrow swept over his face, and he turned away, clenching and unclenching his hands several times.

He didn't know. Dani's mind frantically, desperately jumped to that fact. There was still time for her to make things right, and then, hopefully, to make him understand. "Anton, please, let me explain. . . ."

He turned away. "Come on, everyone," he said, softening his tone as he called to the animals and ignored Dani, "time for bed."

"Anton, please."

He gazed over his shoulder at her, and the look in his eyes chilled her to the bone. "There's nothing left to say, Dani."

The smaller animals skittered toward him, some jumping into baskets set here and there on the ground, others loping up a ramp that led onto a long table set with an array of small cages.

A small brown furry creature skittered past Dani. She screamed, surprised, and jumped away.

Anton threw her a deriding glance and scooped the tiny bundle of fur up into his arms. "Celia, you should watch where you're going."

Anton placed the animal in a cage, then walked to the rock where Clyde was curled. He picked the snake up and set him gently into one of the cages, then turned to urge Isabelle into a large glass terrarium.

How could she make him understand? A sense of loss assailed her, an emptiness invading her heart and aching like nothing she'd ever felt before. This was, she knew suddenly, what she'd feel for the rest of her life if she lost him now. Tears burned her eyes, and she blinked them back. She couldn't let that happen, she couldn't lose him.

A crush of thick ferns to her right rustled loudly, and an alligator broke forth into the clearing. Dani clutched her breast. "Anton," she screamed in warning, and stumbled backward, nearly tripping over a dead tree limb that lay on the ground.

Anton spun around. The huge reptile moved slowly toward him. Dani's heart raced, and she was about to scream again when she noticed the gator had no tail. The reptile croaked as it neared Anton, and Dani realized that the deadly looking jaws held very few teeth. Relief left her almost weak.

"Samson, go on into your pool," Anton said. "I'll bring you some more fish chunks in a while." The gator slid into a pool of water on the other side of the table. "Boris," Anton called. The large cat sauntered toward him, the parrot still perched on his back. "Watch over the others."

Boris roared softly, as if fully understanding what he was supposed to do, and settled down onto the ground before the cages.

Anton refused to talk to her as they walked together back to the house. Rather, he strode through the dense foliage at a purposely brisk pace, rage seeming to surround him like an invisible cloak. Dani skipped, tripped, and ran in an effort to keep up with him and not become lost. The sun was rapidly descending toward the horizon, and the swamp was quickly becoming steeped in shadow.

"Anton, I'm sorry I followed you. Please, let me explain. Just listen."

He strode on without a pause or backward glance.

"I'll never tell another living soul about the animals." But even as she said the words and watched him walk ahead of her, Dani realized, deep down in her heart, that the fury he was exhibiting now was nothing compared to the rage and betrayal he'd feel when he found out the truth about her. She followed him through the foyer, but at his office door he turned abruptly, the gleam of disdain she saw in his eyes as he looked down at her like a touch of ice to her soul. "There's nothing more to say."

She opened her mouth to respond, but he stepped into his office and, before she could follow, slammed the door in her face.

"Anton." Silence met her ears. Tears filled her eyes. Fear invaded her heart. She whirled around and headed for the stairs. There was only one thing left for her to do. In her room she dug the cellular phone out of her bag and dialed Stan's home number. His wife answered, and Dani forced herself to be polite and go through the pleasantries before asking for Stan.

"Whatever you're going to find out for me, Stan, I need it within the next couple of hours."

"Are you crazy?" he bellowed into her ear. "It's night, Dani. Some of us do stop working at night, or haven't you heard?"

She held the phone away from her, and when she heard nothing but silence, returned it to her ear. "I need whatever you can get, Stan, and I need it fast, before I'm thrown out of here."

"He's on to you."

"No, I mean, I don't think so, but close. Anyway, get me whatever else you can on Sandcastle, Pellichet, Tyrene, Knight, the casino, Lexicon, whatever, okay?"

"Call me back later."

Dani changed into a dinner dress, brushed her hair and applied a bit of fresh makeup, and went downstairs, praying with each step she took on the grand staircase that if there were any such thing as a miracle, she could have one now. She hadn't waited twenty-five years to fall in love just to lose it.

Anton nodded to her as she entered the dining room, but that's about all the attention she got from him. He chatted casually with her father over dinner and commented politely to her when he had to. Harlen looked at her questioningly several times during the meal, but Dani did her best to avoid his gaze. She wasn't in the mood for his fatherly sympathy or his competitive arrogance.

Placing her napkin on the table, she rose as soon as Sanitee cleared their plates and brought coffee and dessert. "I think I'll skip dessert," she said, "if you gentlemen will excuse me."

Harlen looked at her in clear puzzlement, knowing her penchant for sweets.

Sanitee stepped into the room from the adjoining door that led to the kitchen. "Mr. Tyrene is on the phone," she said, looking at Anton.

He rose and excused himself.

Dani looked at her father and smiled. "I'm not feeling all that well tonight."

"Me neither. Getting lost in the swamp can do that to a person."

She stared at him, her mouth agape. "You were in the swamp?"

"Yeah, I followed you, but I lost you. Took me a month of Sundays to find my way back, I'll tell you." He chuckled softly. "You almost lost your old man for good this time, kiddo."

Relief flowed through her, not only that he was safe, but that he obviously hadn't seen the animals. Dani smiled. "I'm glad I didn't." She hurried from the dining room and fled up the stairs, shutting and locking her door behind her the moment she stepped into her room. She sat down on the bed and called Stan.

"You're lucky," he growled the moment he recognized her voice. "Just after we talked things began to break. Our hacker traced the hacker who was invading Pellichet's computer files."

"Stan, I should have told you before, but with everything happening I kept getting sidetracked, but I . . ." His words suddenly registered in her brain. "The hacker? He traced the other one?"

"Yep."

She heard the pride in his voice, but was too impatient to acknowledge it. "Who?"

"Carter Tyrene."

"What? That's impossible," Dani said with a gasp.

"It's his office number, Dani. His private number."

"But that would mean Carter is—"

"Trying to screw Reichard."

"Does Carter know we've traced him?"

"We're not sure, but it's possible. After our guy cut the trace, someone tried to hone in on us. But there is another possibility."

"What?"

Stan sighed. "Our guy says it's possible to connect to someone else's line so that the call can't be traced back to your own. Someone could be redirecting their calls through Carter's line in order to cover their tracks."

"Which means it could be anyone," Dani said, feeling suddenly defeated.

"Right. Even Floyd. He could be doing it to frame Carter."

"Or it could be Jim Knight," Dani offered.

"Or half a dozen others," Stan added.

"Stan, check something else for me tonight, would you?"

"Why not? I didn't plan to sleep anyway. And my wife stopped talking to me after I talked to you."

"Check out any connection between Pellichet, Carter, and Jim Knight. And—"

A loud knock on Dani's door cut off her next comment.

"Dani."

She started at Anton's voice, feeling as well as hearing the rage that burned in his tone. Before she could click off the phone or move from the bed, the door slammed open and crashed against the wall.

Anton strode into the room, eyes dark, hair tousled, fists clenched so tightly, his knuckles had paled. "Did you get enough for your story, Miss Coroneaux?" he snarled, his tone dripping with venom. "Or do you need to take a few photocopies of my business files? Which do you prefer? The casino? Lexicon? Or is it the compound you want to write about? Anton Reichard, crazy recluse, retreats to a world of crippled animals because he can't stand being around people anymore. I'm sure you can find some way to make a scandal out of something you've seen here, Miss Coroneaux, your kind always does." He stormed over to the writing desk in the corner of the room, picked up a silver letter opener, and turned back to her, holding it out in offering.

Dani stared, not knowing what to say.

"Why don't you just cut me open now, Dani?" He thrust the letter opener toward her. "Cut out my heart, why don't you? Slice me up, kill me. That's all you and your kind care about anyway . . . scandal, pain, tragedy. It makes for better reading, doesn't it, Dani? Rip someone up, destroy them, and you sell more papers."

Her whole world stopped. He knew who she was. Dani's heart slammed against her rib cage, and a sinking sensation churned within her stomach. Her father had told him after all. Fury fused with despair. She shook her head. "No, Anton, you have to listen, I—"

"Listen?" He threw the letter opener to the floor and, with a few purposeful strides, closed the distance between them, grabbing her arms and dragging her up against his chest. "Listen to what, Dani? More of your lies? How many more do you have to spin?" He laughed harshly, his words clipped with an edge of contempt. His face had become a mask for his rage, controlled, hard, etched with bitterness, while the small scar on his lip stood out against his suddenly ashen pallor like a crimson brand. "That's all this whole thing has been, hasn't it?" he accused. "A lie. Right from the beginning. All of it. Even . . ." His eyes bored cruelly into hers, cold and relentless as death.

Dani tried to blink away the incipient tears that filled her eyes. She couldn't breathe, couldn't look away from him, and couldn't answer, because at that moment she knew, more so than ever before, that the only man she had ever loved, the only man she wanted in her life, was standing in front of her, and she was losing him.

Her gaze moved over his features frantically, looking for some softness of reason, some weakness to his anger. The pale light glowing from the lamp on her nightstand played on his face. It accentuated the straight lines, deepened the shadows that edged each curve, and highlighted the tumble of black hair that had fallen onto his forehead, but revealed no weakening of the rage she felt surrounding him.

She had to make him listen, had to make him understand. Everything had changed. She wasn't the same person she had been when she'd come there. Nothing mattered to her anymore but him and what they'd begun to find together. "Please, Anton, listen to me," Dani implored. "I'm not going to do the story. I mean, I was. When I first came here that's all I cared about, but things changed."

He released her so abruptly, she stumbled back away from him. "Really?" he said with a sneer. "Because you fell for me, right?"

"Yes."

He swore inaudibly, his eyes bitter and hard as he looked at her. Reaching out suddenly, he grabbed Dani again and pulled her to him. His embrace was suffocating, robbing her of breath, but she didn't care. She pressed into him until there was only one shadow on the wall, one heartbeat echoing softly in the silence of the room.

His mouth crushed down atop hers, his kiss harboring no gentleness or care. It was a savage demand, hard and hot, devouring both her passions and her senses. It was a kiss of hunger and need, anger and rejection. His tongue moved around hers, sparring mercilessly, teasing and taunting. Promising everything, promising nothing.

Dani moaned softly, her arms tightening around his shoulders, desperately holding on to him. Relief and anxiety warred within her.

As abruptly as he'd dragged her to him, Anton tore away, pulling himself from her arms and taking a step back, leaving Dani feeling more alone and empty than she remembered ever having felt in her life. He didn't believe her. The thought struck like an icy gale sweeping through her mind. She looked up at him beseechingly. "Anton, you have to believe me," she said softly. "I'd already decided not to do a story on you. I didn't follow you to the compound for that. You have to believe me. I love you."

An ugly laugh erupted from his throat and as quickly died away, leaving his features as hard as stone, his eyes as cold as a New England sea in winter. "Nice touch, Dani, but you forget, I've dealt with reporters before. Though I'll admit that most were not half as beautiful as you, or as good in bed. Is your editor compensating you for that little extra, or was it your own contribution to the story?"

Dani gasped and stared at him in shock, his words having sliced through her and cut straight to her heart. "You . . . you don't mean that."

One dark brow soared arrogantly. "Oh, but I do, Miss Coroneaux. You should be congratulated on your acting skills. And your determination. And here's another thing I mean"—his eyes spit fire as his deep drawl rolled each word with such heavy emphasis that Dani flinched—"I'll expect you out of my house by morning, and, though I realize this is asking a lot from people in your profession, I will expect not to see you here again." Spinning on his heel, he strode down the hall toward the stairs.

"You can't shut everyone out, Anton," Dani said, running to the door and looking after him. "I love you."

He turned to look back at her, then without another word, moved around the corner of the stairs and out of her sight.

Dani stared at the empty hallway, wanting desperately to go after him, and knowing, beyond any doubt, that it wouldn't do any good. She should have told him the truth when they'd made love. No, she should have told him before they'd made love. She should have told him everything. Now it was too late. She moved back into her room and absently began to pace its length. Everything that could go wrong was doing exactly that, and she didn't know what to do. She'd worked long and hard to get where she was in her career, and now she didn't care about it anymore. She didn't care about anything but the man who had just told her to get out of his life.

Dani paused to stare past the open French doors to the grounds beyond, seeing in her mind's eye the small clearing in the bayou where they'd made love.

"Things not going exactly as you'd planned?"

She jerked around, her anger refueled at hearing her father's voice. "Not by a long shot," she snapped, glaring at him. He was leaning casually against the doorjamb and smiling. "But that should make you happy." She walked to the closet and dragged out her suitcase, threw it on the bed, then looked back at him, hatred burning in her eyes. "How could you?" she asked softly, fighting the tears that threatened to overwhelm her. "How could you tell him who I was?"

"I didn't," Harlen said quietly.

Dani turned, eyes narrowed in suspicion. "You're the only other one here who knows. And you're the only other one here who still wants the story."

"That may all be well and true," he said, "but I didn't tell him, even though he let me know in no uncertain terms before coming up here that he's not too pleased that I didn't. He got a phone call from the hospital after you left the dining room, then he stormed out. My guess is Floyd Pellichet is the one who told him."

"Floyd? But how would he know?"

Her father shrugged. "A little checking here and there. It's not hard to break someone's cover, Dani."

She began to throw her things into the suitcase. "It doesn't matter. I'm leaving, and you can have your damned story all to yourself."

"I don't think I want it either."

She whirled around to face him, thoroughly surprised now. "I don't believe you."

He shrugged again. "Your prerogative, but you'd be wrong."

"Why?"

Harlen pushed away from the doorjamb and walked into the room, pausing before Dani. He touched her cheek gently with the tip of one finger. "You love him." It was a statement, not a question. "If there is a story here, and I'm not saying there is, then you're the one who has to do it. You're the only one who can do it, and do it right."

She pulled away from him and slammed a pair of shoes into the suitcase. "I'm not doing a story on Anton. In fact"—she emptied the drawer where she'd put her underwear and tossed them into the bag—"when I get back to the office I'll probably get fired."

"Then quit and do the story freelance. I can help you sell it." He smiled. "There's going to be a lot of publicity about him in the next few months, Dani. Everyone will be doing a story on him, he can't avoid it. Not with the casino opening, and Jim Knight at his throat, looking for revenge. But you can do the right kind of story, because you know the real Reichard."

She shook her head. "He hates publicity. I can't do that to him."

"He may hate it, Dani, but he needs the publicity whether he likes it or not," her father said, "if his clinics are going to survive."

Dani stopped packing and turned to look at him, frowning in puzzlement. "Clinics?"

He nodded. "I told you that I followed you two today." He chuckled. "Got lost once or twice, even fell into that damned mucky water and ruined a very good pair of Loafers, but I caught up to you. And I got back to the house sooner than you two, so I was able to make some phone calls. Not that I didn't already have a hunch about what was going on out here. His sister started it a while back, just before she died. It wasn't public knowledge or big news then, but a few people knew. Then I read about that baby elephant at the Baton Rouge zoo whose mother had rejected it. They couldn't find another to adopt it, and then suddenly the baby was gone. It took me a while, but I finally found a contact who knew a guy whose brother works for the Louisiana zoo and was willing, for a couple of hundred bucks, of course, to talk. That compound of animals Anton keeps out there . . ."

"Yeah?" Dani said, prompting him to continue.

"That's not even the half of it. He funds clinics all over the country, saving animals and finding them new homes."

Dani stared at her father in disbelief, her mouth agape. "And you knew this the whole time? Why didn't you tell me?"

He shrugged. "You were after a different kind of story."

She frowned. "But human interest pieces aren't your thing, Dad. I don't understand. I thought you were here because of the casino, the rumors about Anton pulling out."

"I never figured him to pull out. His background, track record, so to speak, showed that he fights to the end. Doesn't give up."

"So while the rest of us were running around trying to get an angle on a casino scandal or disaster, you were planning this story on him and the animals all along?"

Harlen smiled. "Would have been a real coup, don't you think? Something none of the rest of you even noticed."

Dani laughed and ran to hug her father. "I love you, Dad."

He laughed with her, wrapping his arms around her waist and holding her to him. "I love you too, princess, even if I have been rotten about showing it in the past."

She wiped her tears away when he released her. "But, I don't understand. Shortly after the accident, he cut off all funds to the charities his family had given to for years, without explanation or even comment. The papers damned him for it, remember?"

Harlen nodded.

"Everyone said he'd changed, that he'd become cold, distant, and bitter, that he was out here harboring all the money for himself. They said he blamed everyone else for the accident, and that's why he cut off the funds."

"But nobody really knew the truth," Harlen said. "It was all speculation."

"He needed the money for the animals. For the clinics. That's what he meant about private interests, why he's so upset at the prospect of losing Lexicon." She began to pace, then paused, having decided to fill her father in on everything. "Dad, we've found out that there are financial problems with the casino project. Someone set up a string of dummy contracting companies and has been shoveling money into them, and the trail leads back to Floyd Pellichet."

"So Pellichet's been embezzling."

She shook her head. "I'm not sure. It looks that way, but I saw him when he came here to tell Anton someone was hacking into his computer files on the casino. Dad, the man was really upset, more angry than afraid, and if he had something to hide like embezzlement, I'd think he would be frightened." She scoffed. "Especially of Anton. He'd be the last man Floyd would come to, afraid that Anton was the one behind the file break-in and knew what was happening."

"You think he's being set up?"

Dani's eyes lit up as she whirled to look at her father. "Yes," she said excitedly. "Yes, that has to be it. Stan hired a hacker to try and trace who was hacking into Floyd's files, and he traced the line back to Carter Tyrene's office. We figured Floyd might just be trying to make it look like Carter was breaking into his files, or even that it was Jim Knight trying to put the blame on Carter, but we were wrong."

Now it was Harlen's turn to frown in puzzlement. "Usually I'm pretty good at this stuff, Dani, but I don't follow you."

"Carter was trying to make it look like he's being framed."

"Wouldn't that be kind of dangerous, pointing the finger at himself?"

"Not if it made us suspicious of everyone else." She smiled. "Carter's smart." She remembered another suspicion. "And I don't think he's in this alone. Dad, I have to get into Anton's files. Can you do something to buy me some time? Keep him away from his office?"

"Sure, but what's up?"

She was about to tell a lie, then stopped. He was trying to help her, and if she couldn't trust her own father, who could she trust?

FOURTEEN

Dani grabbed the brass handle and slowly pulled it toward her, cringing at the soft swooshing sound the drawer made as it rolled open. Her father had Anton in the parlor discussing the publicity article Harlen was supposedly doing on the casino, though Dani was still finding it difficult to believe her father was willing to do a story that didn't involve scandal, tragedy, or disaster. She riffled through the folders, grabbing first the ones pertaining to the casino project, then the ones on Lexicon. Finally she found one on the compound, filed simply under the heading "Sherry."

Carrying them to Anton's desk, she flipped through each. If she hadn't known what she was looking for, she'd never have seen it. But she did, and she had. Anton was trying to cover the expenses of the clinics, as well as divert money to the casino project to cover what was being embezzled. He was obviously aware of the betrayal, but not on to who was doing it or how to stop it. Dani returned the folders to the drawer, but frowned as she closed it. There were still loose ends. Jim Knight for one. Where had he gotten the money to buy the Lexicon stock? And was she right about Carter, or was she letting her personal dislike of the man cloud her judgment? Was he actually innocent, and Floyd Pellichet or Jim Knight more devious than she was giving either credit for being?

She had to get to town, talk to Stan, talk to the hacker he had hired, and do a little hacking of her own. She turned off the lamp on Anton's desk and returned to her room. Grabbing her overnight bag, she tossed her makeup into it, along with all of her other toiletries. Her clothes she could get later. Or if things went the way she hoped, it wouldn't matter that she'd left them behind, because she'd be back. She used the back stairs and left the house.

Dani paused on the rear gallery. They'd hear her start her car. She shrugged and dashed around to the front and down the shallow entry stairs. So what? Anton had told her to leave, she was just going tonight instead of waiting until morning.

Anton heard her car start and squelched the urge to run onto the gallery and call her back. She had come to Bayou Noir to dig up a story, a scandal on the casino project and on him, that was all. He'd been a fool to think otherwise, and he refused to continue playing the role. Once he'd been more than willing to lose himself within a woman's wiles, and because of that foolhardiness his family had paid the price. He heard Harlen talking to him but Anton was no longer paying attention. His thoughts had returned to that day almost three years earlier, when his life had suddenly taken a turn toward disaster.

He'd flown his parents and sister, Sherry, to Dallas

so that they could meet with Jim and his family over some last-minute wedding arrangements. They'd only planned on staying a couple of hours, but their conversation had dragged on and on because they couldn't all agree on some minor little detail like reception table compliments. Anton had called Jessica to tell her he might not make their date that night. That had been his first mistake, and the crucial one that had set all of the others into motion. He'd caught her lounging in a tub full of bubbles. By the time she'd gotten through describing what she looked and felt like at the moment, and how hungry she was for him, all in a sultry, seductive voice that had played havoc with both his body and senses, he'd been so hot with desire and determined to get back to New Orleans that it was all he could think of. That's why he'd insisted to his family that they leave Dallas right away, saying he had something important to tend to that couldn't wait. He'd forced them to cut their conversation with the Knights off, and he'd ignored the warnings of a storm coming in from the Gulf.

All he'd thought and cared about was getting back to Jessica and making love to her. But the next time he'd seen her he had been lying in a hospital bed with a badly broken leg, a couple of cracked ribs, a cut lip and shoulder, and his family was dead. Astonishingly, so were all his wild feelings of passion toward Jessica. She'd never understood how he could blame her for the tragedy, and he'd been unable to explain, because he didn't blame her, he blamed himself. She was merely a part of the reason he'd done what he had done, and that was what he had a hard time living with. Whenever he looked at her he saw his own recklessness, his own betrayal.

Anton glanced toward the window and saw the taillights of Dani's car glow red against the night as she drove toward the main road. A sense of loss swept over him, further chilling the loneliness he held around himself, forced upon himself, like a protective cloak of ice. It was better this way. There was no room in his life anymore for that kind of emotion, that kind of trouble. He had the others to think of now. They needed him, depended on him, and this time he wouldn't fail. He turned back to Harlen. "Would you excuse me?" Anton said abruptly, cutting into the other man's conversation.

Harlen nodded and left the room, going up to his own. Anton moved into his study, walked to a cabinet set in the corner, and took a bottle of whiskey from behind one of its elaborately carved doors. Hours later he was still sitting in the room, the bottle half empty. Even with his mind clouded by alcohol, and in spite of the anger and disappointment he still felt toward her, he couldn't dismiss thoughts of Dani from his mind. Her image tormented and called to him, and Anton knew then that it always would, that now he had another ghost to add to those already haunting him.

ƒ Dani sat on the floor of her office, surrounded by the printouts the hacker had pulled from Floyd Pellichet's computer files. Interspersed among those papers were copies of everything else Stan had come up with on Anton's business and personal life since the accident, along with the notes she'd gathered while looking through Anton's files. She had read every page more than a dozen times, and sorted them into chronological order. Her suspicion that the embezzlement and Jim Knight's sudden influx of enough money to buy stock in Lexicon were connected was right. There was no getting around the matching numbers.

Stan walked into the room, looked around, then peered over her shoulder at the scratch pad she'd been making notes on. "Pellichet checked himself out of the hospital a few hours ago."

Dani turned to look up at him, then glanced back at her notepad, tapping her pencil on it. "They're connected, Stan," Dani said. "The embezzlement and Jim Knight's sudden availability of funds. But why did Floyd, or Carter, whichever is our real embezzler, want Knight to buy Lexicon stock?"

"Divert Reichard's attention from the casino? Keep him from catching on to the fake companies until it was too late?"

Dani nodded. "Stan, is anyone watching Pellichet?"

"No, why?"

"Because if he's our man he's going to leave. He'd probably be gone already if he hadn't been in that accident."

Stan grabbed the phone. "I'll get someone on him."

An hour later the man Stan ordered to check on Floyd Pellichet called in. Floyd was home and didn't seem to be planning to go anywhere. In fact, he'd made himself comfortable in his sunroom and was taking a nap.

"That doesn't make sense," Dani snapped, frustrated.

"Maybe it does," Stan mused.

"You want to run that past me again?"

"Think about it," Stan said. "At first we thought Floyd was afraid Anton was catching on to his embezzling scheme with Sandcastle and the defunct companies and had tried to divert suspicion from himself by making it look like someone was trying to hack into his computer files on the casino. Right?"

"Yeah?"

"Then we found out it was Carter Tyrene, or someone in his office, who was doing the hacking. But every personal and financial check we've done on Carter came back clean, as did every one on Jim Knight, so we began to look at Floyd again." Stan smiled, running a fleshy hand over his bald pate. "And maybe that's exactly what our man wants, for us to be watching Floyd."

"Sanitee has to be in on this," Dani said, suddenly turning the conversation in a new direction.

"The housekeeper?" Stan asked, puzzled. "Why?"

"Because I think whoever's behind this had to have full access to Anton and his files in order to keep tabs on whether he was getting suspicious, so that if he did, they'd know how much time they had left before they had to run. His previous secretary is dead, and we know I didn't do it. That leaves Sanitee."

"Makes sense."

"Sanitee would have known Anton was becoming suspicious of those companies. She most likely even saw his notes on them." Dani stiffened, suddenly realizing the significance of something she hadn't thought much of. "And she was meeting a man on the plantation at night, after she thought everyone else was asleep."

"Who?"

"I don't know. I didn't think it was that important to trace the housekeeper's lover. Obviously I was wrong."

"Yeah, well, sneaking off to meet a man at night isn't proof of embezzlement," Stan said.

A young copy editor stuck his head through the doorway. "Mr. Gates, Mr. Pierce is here."

Dani frowned.

"The hacker," Stan said, and she nodded.

For the next twenty minutes she rattled off numbers she'd accumulated from the files. Seconds later their hacker found the exact same amount of money deposited in a bank account. Over the next hour they discovered a dozen other accounts set up around town with a dozen different banks, all under the same two names, Harrison C. and Sanitee Tyrene.

Dani grabbed the file of background checks Stan had accumulated over the past two days and pulled out one on Carter. "Harrison C. was Carter's father," she said. "And he's dead." She snatched up the phone and dialed the plantation. "Yes, this is Mzzz. Smithers, with Mr. Harlen Coroneaux's office," she said in a faked, squeaky voice when Sanitee answered. "May I speak with him puh—leeze?"

A moment later Dani's father was on the line. "Dad, don't say anything, it's me," Dani said hurriedly. "Listen, I'm on my way back. Is Anton still in the parlor?"

"No," Harlen said.

Dani hated guessing games. "Has he gone to bed?"

"No, Ms. Smithers, you were actually closer to being right the first time."

"In his study?" Dani asked.

"Yes."

"Good. Keep him there and don't let Sanitee or Carter anywhere near him or his files, okay? If I can get him to listen to me, I think I can explain what's been happening, and who's behind it. Stan's still checking on things, but I think the police will be able to find the proof they need once we tell them what we've found."

"I understand, Ms. Smithers, yes. Good-bye."

As she was about to hang up, Dani heard another soft click echo through the line. She turned to the hacker. "I think if you keep checking, you'll come up with some money transfers that will explain how Jim Knight's failing stocks suddenly began paying dividends."

"Yeah," Stan muttered, "no doubt. You think he's partners in this with Tyrene?"

She jumped up and grabbed her purse. "Maybe, but I'd bet he's just being used, like Floyd, to divert attention from the fact that Carter is bleeding the casino project dry."

"What are you going to do?"

"Tell Anton."

"You think he'll believe you?"

"He has to." She paused at the door and looked back at him, knowing the time was long past to say what she'd been intending to say for days. "Stan, I'm not going to do the casino story on Anton. I can't."

"Don't decide that now, Dani," he said softly. "But think about it. Somebody's going to do it, and who better to do him justice in the news than the woman who loves him?"

Stan's words echoed through Dani's mind as she drove toward Bayou Noir, and in spite of the fact that she wished she could think of some way to protect Anton from the press altogether, she knew Stan was right. Somebody was going to do this story, and she knew it better than anyone, could do it better than anyone.

But if she did, would she lose Anton?

❖————————❖

Dani pulled the car onto the plantation's shelled drive but didn't slow. Getting to Anton quickly seemed more important than ever now. "He has to listen," she mumbled to herself, remembering that second click she'd heard on the phone line after talking with her father. She wondered now if that had been Anton, and he already knew what she had to say.

A frown tugged at her brow as an ugly thought tugged at her mind. Could Anton already know about everything because he was behind it? The embezzling? The fake companies? Were his other businesses in trouble, or the clinics, and he was diverting money from the casino project for himself?

Memory of being wrapped in his arms, of his lips crushed against hers, his nearness filling her with an ecstasy like she'd never known, danced through Dani's head, taunting her and turning her blood hot with need for him. She almost laughed aloud at the absurdity of her suspicions, and flung them from her thoughts. Anton Reichard had invaded the very essence of her being, instilled her with a need to be loved by him, a desire to spend the rest of her life with him, that was stronger than she could control or deny. She loved him, and if she had to face down the world for him, she would not lose him.

She pulled the Mustang up in front of the house and, killing the engine, jumped out of the car, not noticing until that moment that no light shone in any of the windows of the house.

"He's not here."

The voice came to her out of the darkness, startling

her so abruptly that she nearly threw herself back into the car. At the last second before panic gripped her she recognized the voice as her father's, released the death grip she'd secured on the door, and sighed audibly.

He stepped out of the shadows of the wide gallery, and she saw the burning tip of his cigar glow red against the blackness of the night.

"What do you mean he's not here?" she finally managed, trembling.

"I think he's at the compound. After you left he practically ordered me out of the parlor, then closed himself up in his study and drank himself into a half stupor. I tried to join him there after your call, but he wouldn't let me in. He left about an hour ago. I was sitting here"—he motioned to one of the tall wicker chairs that graced the front gallery—"having a smoke before going to bed. I tried to stop him and nearly got a fist in my nose for the trouble." He moved toward her. "What did you find out?"

"We believe Carter's been embezzling from the casino funds and trying to frame Floyd Pellichet. Stan's still working on it, but I think we've got enough to point the police in the right direction."

Harlen nodded. "Don't tell me anymore, Dani. It's your story." He smiled, and moved from the gallery to the shallow entry steps. Moonlight touched each craggy line of his face and turned his gray locks to shimmering threads of silver.

Dani looked over her shoulder toward the bayou. A shudder crawled through her at the thought of going in there alone, especially at night, but she knew she had to go. She looked back at her father. "Where's Sanitee?"

"She drove off just after Anton left the house."

Dani stared at him. "The second click," she mumbled.

"The what?" Harlen asked.

"I've got to get to Anton."

Harlen frowned. "You can't go in the bayou alone, Dani. It's dangerous."

"I'll take Lady Jane," she said, deciding being mounted on the horse was much safer and preferable to walking. And the horse knew her way home if they got lost. "Call Stan and tell him I think Sanitee overheard our phone conversation. She's probably picking up Carter now and heading for the airport."

Thankfully, she'd remembered to bring a flashlight. Dani shone the beam of light ahead of her and instantly jerked back on the reins as her face came within inches of colliding with a huge spiderweb. Her heart thudded madly. She'd been crazy to come out alone in the dark and expect to find the compound.

A low growl emitted from beneath a bush to her left. Dani swallowed the whimper of fear that wanted desperately to break from her throat, and nudged her knees into Lady Jane's sides, urging the horse back into movement.

"Freddy loves Boris. Squawk!"

Dani reined in again, instantly recognizing the parrot's patter and thinking she'd never heard anything so beautiful in all of her life. Except, she realized instantly, that Freddy was most likely accompanied by Boris, who was several hundred pounds of muscle, claws, and fangs. Dani shivered at the mere thought, but steeled herself not to turn and flee. She had to find Anton. "Freddy?" she called softly. "Freddy, where are you?"

"Freddy?" the parrot mimicked. "Freddy, where are you? Freddy loves Boris."

She urged Lady Jane forward, and within seconds the tall iron gate of the compound came into view, each black rod glistening a reflection of the full moon that was shining down on the bayou that night. Freddy was sitting on the top of the gate, and his friend Boris was nowhere in sight. Dani sighed in relief. Sliding from the saddle, she led Lady Jane into the compound until they came to the clearing. Anton stood beside the row of small cages, bent over the table, intent on bandaging the leg of what appeared to be a wounded raccoon. He looked up as Lady Jane nickered.

Dani saw the anger that swept into his eyes. Glancing hurriedly over her shoulder to make certain that the horse was okay with being surrounded by a menagerie of other creatures, and seeing that she was, Dani crossed the clearing. "Please, you have to listen to me," she said.

He straightened and set the raccoon aside. "You don't have anything to say that I want to hear, Miss Coroneaux."

"I know who betrayed you."

"So do I." His gaze bored into hers.

She felt like withering under the accusatory glare. Instead, Dani threw back her shoulders and gave him glare for glare. "I mean I know who's been embezzling money from the casino project and how."

His eyes narrowed, but he remained silent, waiting.

"I thought it was Floyd, and that he was only trying to throw suspicion away from himself, but then I started looking at Carter and—"

"Carter?"

"Yes. But that didn't seem right either, so I checked out Jim Knight, and, of course, that was wrong."

"I thought you said you knew who it was."

"I do." She started over, slowly, running each detail she'd discovered past him. Half an hour later she stopped talking. "So you see, Carter was really quite ingenious. He was making it look like Floyd was trying to frame him so that it would seem that much more that Floyd was the guilty one. Carter set up all those fake companies under Sandcastle, and Sandcastle under Floyd's name. He diverted funds from some of it to Jim Knight's account and made certain Jim got the word that if he really wanted to hurt you, he could do it by buying up Lexicon stock."

"How?" Anton challenged.

"Well, I don't know that, but I'm sure it wouldn't be hard to find out. Maybe a crooked investment counselor or something. Or maybe he even told Jim himself, who knows?"

Anton nodded and held out his hand. "I guess I owe you an apology, Miss Coroneaux. You're a better reporter than I'd thought. Will the story be on page one tomorrow?"

Dani stared at his hand. He was offering it as if the gesture was no more than a business formality. A simple hello or good-bye. She felt her world slipping away from her, out of her control, and she mentally grappled to snatch it back. Her gaze shot back up to meet his, blue fusing with blue, daring, probing, questioning, hesitating.

Anton was the first to break the spell that seemed to be holding them together. He stepped back, ripping his

gaze from hers. "Will your story be on page one tomorrow?"

"I'm not doing the story. I told my boss earlier that I
wouldn't."

But instead of the relief, or even happiness, she
thought she'd see on his face at her words, he merely
shrugged. "It doesn't matter. Someone else will."

Those were the same words Stan had said to her.

"I'll see you back to the house."

Dani stiffened. That was it then. She'd lost him.
Blinking at the tears that threatened to come to her eyes,
she turned and walked toward Lady Jane.

Behind her, Anton called to the animals, ushering
them to their beds.

Dani turned back and watched him. This was his
world, the one he'd created in memory of his sister, and
for himself, and she obviously had no part in it. She
reached for Lady Jane's reins and felt something warm
and soft brush up against her leg. Startled, she jumped
back, shrieking softly as she looked down. Boris stared
up at her, the saddest expression she'd ever seen glistening from within the small brown eyes that suddenly
looked older than time. As Dani trembled, the lion
closed the short distance between them and rubbed his
bushy mane against her hip gently, yet firmly enough so
that she felt the nudge he gave her, forcing her to take a
step toward Anton.

"Leave her alone, Boris," Anton commanded, "and
go to bed."

The big cat ignored him and rubbed against Dani
again, this time emitting a low, rumbling growl that
Dani, even through the stark terror she was feeling at
being so close to the lion, knew instantly was not a threat

but a plea. That realization suddenly chased the fear away.

"He doesn't want me to leave," she said, summoning every ounce of courage she could find in herself to face Anton again.

"He doesn't know what he wants except to be fed and petted," Anton said, and closed Clyde's cage.

"He knows what I want," Dani said. She met Anton's gaze, then walked toward him when he didn't move. "He knows I want you. And I think he knows that you want me."

"There's nothing here for you, Dani," Anton said coldly. "Look around." He waved an arm at their surroundings. "Every creature here frightens you. Even my sister's cat scares you, and Pichouette wouldn't harm a flea."

"I'm not afraid of Pichouette anymore. We're friends."

"Good. But this is my world, Dani, and you don't belong in it."

She felt his rejection cut straight to her heart, but she refused to accept it. Not yet. Not until she really believed that he meant it. That he didn't love her.

Praying for strength and courage, she tentatively reached out to touch the head of the huge cat who still sat beside her. When he closed his eyes, leaned into her, and purred, sounding more like a runaway train than a cat, Dani smiled and, stroking Boris's head tenderly with her hand, turned her gaze back to Anton. "I do belong here," she said softly. "With you." She looked around. "And with them."

He stood still, watching her, not daring to move or speak, or even hope. The loneliness had been with him for so long, the cold self-hatred and guilt, that he wasn't certain that he could let them go now, that he had a right to let them go and to love her. Anton turned away. "It won't work," he said softly.

She paused and stared at him, waiting for him to go on, praying that when he did she would be able to find the right words to convince him that all she wanted was him.

He turned back, his eyes hard and distant as he stared down at her. "Our lives are too different."

She smiled. "A few months ago, even a few weeks ago, I would have agreed, but that was before I came to know you." She closed the distance between them and reached up to gently touch his cheek with the tips of her fingers. "That was before I fell in love with you." Dani looked around at all the creatures that surrounded them, their innocent eyes watching. "And with them," she added softly.

Rising onto her toes, Dani pressed her lips to his, and when she felt his arms move around her, pulling her close, crushing her to his body, she smiled.

EPILOGUE

Harlen Coroneaux sat back in his chair and stared at the front page of the newspaper. On it were three separate stories concerning what had happened at Bayou Noir over the last couple of days. Dani had written the headliner, which was the one concerning the casino embezzlement. Carter and Sanitee Tyrene had been picked up by the police when they got to the airport, just about the time Dani had returned to the house with Anton the night before. All of the money had been recovered, except that funneled to Jim Knight, but in actuality that had been returned too. The police had explained to Jim that Carter had been using him to ruin Anton, but at first Jim Knight had only laughed and said too bad it hadn't worked. Then Harlen had taken him aside and explained about the clinics that Anton had established in Sherry's memory, and he'd tearfully turned all of his shares in Lexicon back over to Anton.

Harlen had been asked to write a piece for the *Picayune*, and he'd gladly obliged. He reread the story on Sherry Reichard and her brother's ongoing determination to continue with her dream of opening more and more clinics until every animal everywhere had a home and care, no matter how old, injured, or feeble.

Stan Gates had written the last column, and it was the one that brought both a tear to Harlen's eye and a smile to his lips. Tony Reichard and Dani Coroneaux had announced their engagement and would be flying to Paris that afternoon to be married.

Rising from his chair, Harlen picked up the telephone and called home. "Gladys," he said when Dani's mother answered, "pack your best dress, sweetheart. We've got a wedding to go to."

THE EDITORS' CORNER

Begin your holiday celebration early with the four new LOVESWEPT romances coming your way next month. Packed with white-hot emotion, each of these novels is the best getaway from the hustle and bustle typical of this time of year. So set aside a few hours for yourself, cuddle up with the books, and enjoy!

THE DAMARON MARK: THE LION, LOVESWEPT #814, is the next enticing tale in Fayrene Preston's bestselling Damaron Mark series. Lion Damaron is too gorgeous to be real, a walking heartbreaker leaning against a wrecked sports car, when Gabi St. Armand comes to his rescue! She doesn't dare let his seductive smile persuade her he is serious, but flirting with the wealthy hunk is reckless fun—and the only way she can disguise the desire that scorches her very soul. Fayrene Preston beguiles once more with her irresistible tale of unexpected, impossible love that simply must be.

TALL, DARK, AND BAD is the perfect description for the hero in Charlotte Hughes's newest LOVESWEPT, #815. He storms her grandmother's dinner party like a warrior claiming his prize, but when Cooper Garrett presses Summer Pettigrew against the nearest wall and captures her mouth, she has no choice but to surrender. He agrees to play her fiancé in a breathless charade, but no game of let's pretend can be this steamy, this erotic. Get set for a story that's both wickedly funny and wildly arousing, as only Charlotte Hughes can tell it.

For her holiday offering, Peggy Webb helps Santa decide who's **NAUGHTY AND NICE**, #816. Benjamin Sullivan III knows trouble when he spots it in a redhead's passionate glare, but figuring out why Holly Jones is plotting against the town's newest arrival is a mystery too fascinating to ignore! How can she hunger so for a handsome scoundrel? Holly wonders, even as she finds herself charmed, courted, and carried away by Ben's daredevil grin. Award-winning author Peggy Webb makes mischief utterly sexy and wins hearts with teasing tenderness!

Suzanne Brockmann's seductive and inventive romance tangles readers in **THE KISSING GAME**, LOVESWEPT, #817. Allowing Simon Hunt to play her partner on her latest assignment probably isn't Frankie Paresky's best idea ever, but the P.I. finds it just as hard as most women do to tell him no! When a chase to solve a long-ago mystery sparks a sizzling attraction between old friends, Frankie wavers between pleasure and panic. Simon's the best bad boy she's ever known, and he just might turn out to be the man she'll always love. Suzanne Brockmann delivers pure pleasure from the first page to the last.

Happy reading!

With warmest wishes,

Beth de Guzman

Shauna Summers

Beth de Guzman   Shauna Summers

Senior Editor   Editor

P.S. Watch for these Bantam women's fiction titles coming in December: Join *New York Times* bestselling author Sandra Brown for **BREAKFAST IN BED**, available in mass-market. Kay Hooper, nationally bestselling author of *AMANDA*, weaves a tale of mystery when two strangers are drawn together by one fatal moment in **AFTER CAROLINE**. The long-out-of-print classic **LOVE'S A STAGE**, by the beloved writing team Sharon and Tom Curtis, is back for your pleasure. And for her Bantam Books debut, Patricia Coughlin presents **LORD SAVAGE**. Don't miss the previews of these exceptional novels in next month's LOVESWEPTs.

If you're into the world of computers and would like current information on Bantam's women's fiction, visit our Web site, ISN'T IT ROMANTIC, at the following address: **http://www.bdd.com/ romance.**

And immediately following this page, sneak a peek at the Bantam women's fiction titles on sale *now*!

Don't miss these extraordinary titles
by your favorite Bantam authors!

On sale in October:

SHADOWS AND LACE
by Teresa Medeiros

THE MARRIAGE WAGER
by Jane Ashford

She was a slave to his passion . . . but he was
the master of her heart

SHADOWS
AND LACE

a stunning novel of captive love
by national bestseller

Teresa Medeiros

*With one roll of the dice, the shameful deed was done.
Baron Lindsey Fordyce had gambled and lost, and now his
beautiful daughter, Rowena, was about to pay the price.
Spirited away to an imposing castle, the fiery innocent
found herself pressed into the service of a dark and forbidding knight accused of murder . . . and much more.
Handsome, brooding Sir Gareth of Caerleon had spent
years waiting for this chance for revenge. But when he
sought to use the fair Rowena to slay the ghosts of his
tortured past, he never imagined he'd be ensnared in a
silken trap of his own making—slave to a desire he could
never hope to quench. . . .*

Rowena came bursting in like a ray of sunshine cutting through the stale layer of smoke that hung over
the hall. The wild, sweet scent of the moor clung to
her hair, her skin, the handwoven tunic she wore. Her

cheeks were touched with the flushed rose of exertion; her eyes were alight with exuberance.

She ran straight to her father, her words tumbling out faster than the apples dumped from the sack she clutched upside down.

"Oh, Papa, I am ever so happy you've come home! Where did you have the stallion hidden? He is the most beautiful animal I ever saw. Did you truly find your elusive fortune this journey?"

Falling to her knees beside his chair, she pulled a crumpled bunch of heather from her pocket and dumped it in his lap without giving him time to reply.

"I brought your favorite flowers and Little Freddie has promised to cook apples on the coals. They will be hot and sweet and juicy, just as you like them. 'Twill be a hundred times better than any nasty old roasted hare. Oh, Papa, you're home! We thought you were never coming back."

She threw her arms around his waist. The uninhibited gesture knocked the cap from her head to unleash a cascade of wheaten curls.

Fordyce's arms did not move to encircle her. He sat stiff in her embrace. She lifted her face, aware of a silence broken only by the thump of a log shifting on the fire. Her father did not meet her eyes, and for one disturbing moment, she thought she saw his lower lip tremble.

She followed his gaze. Her brothers stood lined up before the hearth in the most ordered manner she had ever seen them. Irwin beamed from the middle of the row.

Bathed in the light of the flickering fire, the stranger stepped out of the shadows. Rowena raised her eyes. From where she knelt, it was as if she was peering up from the bottom of a deep well to meet the eyes of the man who towered over her. His level gaze sent a bolt of raw fear through her, riveting her to the floor as she stared into the face of death itself. A long moment passed before she could pull her eyes away.

"Papa?" she breathed, patting his cool, trembling hand.

He stroked her hair, his eyes distant. "Rowena, I believe 'twould be fitting for you to step outside till we have concluded our dealings."

"You made no mention of a daughter, Fordyce." The stranger's gaze traveled between father and child.

Papa's arm curved around Rowena's shoulders like a shield. The stranger's mocking laughter echoed through the hall. Only Rowena heard Papa's muttered curse as he realized what he had done.

"Your interest is in my sons," Papa hissed, a tiny vein in his temple beginning to throb.

"But *your* interest is not. That much is apparent."

The man advanced and Rowena rose, knowing instinctively that she did not want to be on her knees at this stranger's feet. She stood without flinching to face the wrought links of the silver chain mail that crossed the man's chest. From broad shoulders to booted feet, his garments were as black as the eyes that regarded her with frank scrutiny. She returned his perusal with arms crossed in front of her.

A closer look revealed his eyes were not black, but a deep, velvety brown. Their opacity rendered them inscrutable, but alive with intelligence. Heavy, arched brows added a mocking humor that gave Rowena the impression she was being laughed at, although his expression did not waver. His sable hair was neatly cut, but an errant waviness warned of easy rebellion. His well-formed features were saved from prettiness by an edge of rugged masculinity enhanced by his sheer size. The thought flitted through Rowena's mind that he might be handsome if his face was not set in such ruthless lines.

He reached down and lifted a strand of her hair as if hypnotized at its brightness. The velvety tendril curled around his fingers at the caress.

Rowena's hand slipped underneath her tunic, but before she could bring the knife up to strike, her wrist was twisted in a fearful grip that sent the blade clattering to the stones. She bit her lip to keep from crying out. The man loosed her.

"She has more fire than the rest of you combined." The stranger strode back to the hearth. "I'll take her."

The hall exploded in enraged protest. Papa sank back in the chair, his hand over his eyes.

"You cannot have my sister!" Little Freddie's childish tenor cut through his brothers' cries.

The man leaned against the hearth with a smirk. "Take heart, lad. 'Tis not forever. She is only to serve me for a year."

Rowena looked at Papa. His lips moved with no sound. Her brothers spewed forth dire and violent threats, although they remained in place as if rooted to the stone. She wondered if they had all taken leave of their senses. The stranger's sparkling eyes offered no comfort. They watched her as if delighting in the chaos he had provoked. The tiny lines around them crinkled as he gave her a wink made all the more threatening by its implied intimacy. A primitive thrill of fear shot through her, freezing her questions before they could leave her lips.

Papa's whine carried just far enough to reach the man's ears. "We said sons, did we not?"

The man's booming voice silenced them all. "Nay, Fordyce. We said children. I was to have the use of one of your children for a year."

Rowena's knees went as slack as her jaw. Only the sheer effort of her will kept her standing.

"You cannot take a man's only daughter," said Papa, unable to keep the pleading note from his voice. "Show me some mercy, won't you?"

The knight snorted. "Mercy? What have you ever known of mercy, Fordyce? I've come to teach you of justice."

Papa mustered his courage and banged with force on the arm of the chair. "I will not allow it."

The stranger's hand went to the hilt of the massive sword sheathed at his waist. Beneath the rich linen of his surcoat, the muscles in his arms rippled with the slight gesture. "You choose to fight?" he asked softly.

Lindsey Fordyce hesitated the merest moment. "Rowena, you must accompany this nice man."

Rowena blinked stupidly, thrown off guard by her father's abrupt surrender.

Little Freddie charged forward, an iron pot wielded over his head like a bludgeon. The knight turned with sword drawn. Rowena lunged for his arm, but Papa sailed past both of them and knocked the boy to the ground with a brutal uppercut. Freddie glared at his father, blood trickling from his mouth and nose.

"Don't be an idiot," Papa spat. "He will only kill you, and then he will kill me."

Still wielding his sword, the stranger faced the row of grumbling boys. "If anyone cares to challenge my right to their sister, I shall be more than happy to defend it."

The broad blade gleamed in the firelight. Big Freddie returned the man's stare for a long moment, his callused paws clenched into fists. He turned away and rested his forehead against the warm stones of the hearth.

The stranger's eyes widened as Irwin's plump form stepped forward, trumpet still clutched in hand. Papa took one step toward Irwin, who then plopped his ample bottom on the hearth and studied the trumpet as if seeing it for the first time.

"A wager is a wager." Papa ran his thumbs along the worn gilt of his tattered surcoat. "As you well know, I am a baron and a knight myself—an honorable man."

He sighed as if the burden of his honor was too much for him to bear. The short laugh uttered by the knight was not a pleasant sound.

Papa gently took Rowena's face between his moist palms. "Go with him, Rowena." He swallowed with difficulty. "He will not harm you."

The stranger watched the exchange in cryptic silence, his arms crossed over his chest.

Rowena searched her father's face, blindly hoping for a burst of laughter to explain away the knight's intrusion as a cruel jest. The hope that flickered within her sputtered and died, smothered by the bleakness in the cornflower-blue eyes that were a pale, rheumy echo of her own.

"I shall go with him, Papa, if you say I should."

The man moved forward, unlooping the rope at his waist. Papa stepped back to keep a healthy sword's distance away from the imposing figure.

Rowena shoved her hands behind her back. "There is no need to bind me."

The man retrieved her hands. Rowena did not

flinch as he bound her wrists in front of her none too gently.

Her soft tone belied her anger. "If Papa says I am to go with you, then I will go."

The dark head remained bowed as he tightened the knot with a stiff jerk. Coiling the free end of the rope around his wrist, he led her to the door without a word. She slowed to scoop up her cap. Feeling the sudden tautness in the rope, the man tugged. Rowena dug her heels into the flagstones, resisting his pull. Their eyes met in a silent battle of wills. Without warning, he yanked the rope, causing Rowena to stumble. She straightened, her eyes shining with angry tears for an instant. Then their blue depths cleared and she purposefully followed him through the door, cap clutched in bound hands.

The boys shuffled after them like the undead in a grim processional. Papa meandered behind. Little Freddie was gripped between two of his brothers; a fierce scowl darkened his fair brow.

Night had fallen. A full moon cast its beams through the scant trees, suffusing the muted landscape with the eerie glow of a bogus daylight. Big Freddie gave a low, admiring whistle as a white stallion seemed to rise from the thin shroud of mist that cloaked the ground. The fog entwined itself around the graceful fetlocks. The creature pranced nervously at the sound of approaching footsteps.

Rowena's eyes were drawn to the golden bridle crowning the massive animal. Jewels of every hue encrusted its length. Why would a man of such wealth come all the way to Revelwood to steal a poor man's child? The knight's forbidding shoulders invited no questions as he mounted the horse and slipped Rowena's tether over the leather pommel. The horse's iron-shod hooves twitched. How close could she follow without being pounded to a pulp?

Irwin stepped in front of the horse as if accustomed to placing his bulk in the path of a steed mounted by a fully armed nobleman. The knight leaned back in the saddle with a sigh.

"Kind sir?" Irwin's voice was a mere squeak, so he cleared his throat and tried again. "Kind sir, I hasten to remind you that you are stealing away our only ray of light in a life of darkness. You pluck the single bloom in our garden of grim desolation. I speak for all of us."

Irwin's cousins looked at one another and scratched their heads. Rowena wished faintly that the knight would run him through and end her embarrassment.

"You make an eloquent plea, lad," the knight replied, surprising them all. "Mayhaps you should plead with her father to make his wagers with more care in the future."

From behind Big Freddie, Papa dared to shoot the man a look of pure hatred.

"You will not relent?" asked Irwin.

"I will not."

"Then I pray the burden of chivalry rests heavily on your shoulders. I pray you will honor my sweet cousin with the same consideration you would grant to the rest of the fair and weaker sex."

Rowena itched to box his ears, remembering the uncountable times she had wrestled him to the ground and pinched him until he squealed for mercy.

The stranger again uttered that short, unpleasant laugh. "Do not fear, lad. I will grant her the same consideration that I would grant to any wench as comely as she. Now stand aside or be trampled."

Irwin tripped to the left as the knight kicked the stallion into a trot. Rowena broke into a lope to avoid being jerked off her feet. She dared break her concentration only long enough for one last hungry look at her family. She heard the soft thud of fist pummeling flesh and a familiar cry as Little Freddie tackled Irwin in blind rage and frustration.

Then they were gone. She focused all of her attention on the rocky turf beneath her feet as her world narrowed to the task of putting one foot in front of the other without falling nose first into the drumming hooves.

THE MARRIAGE WAGER

by

Jane Ashford

After watching her husband gamble his life away, Lady Emma Tarrant was determined to prevent another young man from meeting a similar fate. So she challenged the scoundrel who held his debts to another game. After eight years of war, Colin Wareham thought he'd seen it all, but when Lady Emma accosted him, he was suddenly intrigued—and aroused. So he named his stakes: a loss, and he'd forgive the debts. A win, and the lady must give him her heart. . . .

"Will you discard, sir?"

He looked as if he wished to speak, but in the end he simply laid down a card. Focusing on her hand, Emma tried to concentrate all her attention upon it. But she was aware now of his gaze upon her, of his compelling presence on the other side of the table.

She looked up again. He *was* gazing at her, steadily, curiously. But she could find no threat in his eyes. On the contrary, they were disarmingly friendly. He could not possibly look like that and wish her any harm, Emma thought dreamily.

He smiled.

Emma caught her breath. His smile was amazing—warm, confiding, utterly trustworthy. She must have misjudged him, Emma thought.

"Are you sure you won't have some of this excellent brandy?" he asked, sipping from his glass. "I really can recommend it."

Seven years of hard lessons came crashing back upon Emma as their locked gaze broke. He was doing this on purpose, of course. Trying to divert her attention, beguile her into making mistakes and losing. Gathering all her bitterness and resolution, Emma shifted her mind to the cards. She would not be caught so again.

Emma won the second hand, putting them even. But as she exulted in the win, she noticed a small smile playing around Colin Wareham's lips and wondered at it. He poured himself another glass of brandy and sipped it. He looked as if he was thoroughly enjoying himself, she thought. And he didn't seem at all worried that she might beat him. His arrogance was infuriating.

All now rested on the third hand. As she opened a new pack of cards and prepared to deal, Emma took a deep breath.

"You are making a mistake, refusing this brandy," Colin said, sipping again.

"I have no intention of fuzzing my wits with drink," answered Emma crisply. She did not look at him as she snapped out the cards.

"Who are you?" he said abruptly. "Where do you come from? You have the voice and manner of a nobleman's daughter, but you are nothing like the women I meet in society."

Emma flushed a little. There was something in his tone—it might be admiration or derision—that made her self-conscious. Let some of those women spend the last seven years as she had, she thought bitterly, and then see what they were like. "I came here to play cards," she said coldly. "I have said I do not wish to converse with you."

Raising one dark eyebrow, he picked up his hand. The fire hissed in the grate. One of the candles guttered, filling the room with the smell of wax and smoke. At this late hour, the streets outside were silent; the only sounds were Ferik's surprisingly delicate snores from the hall.

In silence, they frowned over discards and calculated odds. Finally, after a long struggle, Wareham said, "I believe this point is good." He put down a card.

Emma stared at it.

"And also my quint," he added, laying down another.

Emma's eyes flickered to his face, then down again.

"Yes?" he urged.

Swallowing, she nodded.

"Ah. Good. Then—a quint, a tierce, fourteen aces, three kings, and eleven cards played, ma'am."

Emma gazed at the galaxy of court cards which he spread before her, then fixed on the one card he still held. The game depended on it, and there was no hint to tell her what she should keep to win the day. She hesitated a moment longer, then made her decision. "A diamond," she said, throwing down the rest of her hand.

"Too bad," he replied, exhibiting a small club.

Emma stared at the square of pasteboard, stunned. She couldn't believe that he had beaten her. "Piqued, repiqued, and capotted," she murmured. It was a humiliating defeat for one with her skill.

"Bad luck."

"I cannot believe you kept that club."

"Rather than throw it away on the slender chance of picking up an ace or a king?"

Numbly, Emma nodded. "You had been taking such risks."

"I sometimes bet on the slim chances," he conceded. "But you must vary your play if you expect to keep your opponent off-balance." He smiled.

That charming smile, Emma thought. Not gloating or contemptuous, but warm all the way to those extraordinary eyes. It almost softened the blow of losing. Almost.

"We said nothing of your stake for this game," he pointed out.

"You asked me for none," Emma retorted. She could not nearly match the amount of Robin Bellingham's notes.

"True." He watched as she bit her lower lip in frustration, and savored the rapid rise and fall of her breasts under the thin bodice of her satin gown. "It appears we are even."

She pounded her fist softly on the table. She had been sure she could beat him, Colin thought. And she had not planned beyond that point. He waited, curious to see what she would do now.

She pounded the table again, thwarted determination obvious in her face. "Will you try another match?" she said finally.

A fighter, Colin thought approvingly. He breathed in the scent of her perfume, let his eyes linger on the creamy skin of her shoulders. He had never encountered such a woman before. He didn't want her to go. On the contrary, he found himself wanting something quite different. "One hand," he offered. "If you win, the notes are yours."

"And if I do not?" she asked.

"You may still have them, but I get . . ." He hesitated. He was not the sort of man who seduced young ladies for sport. But she had come here to his house and challenged him, Colin thought. She was no schoolgirl. She had intrigued and irritated and roused him.

"What?" she said rather loudly.

He had been staring at her far too intensely, Colin realized. But the brandy and the strangeness of the night had made him reckless. "You," he replied.

On sale in November:

AFTER CAROLINE
by Kay Hooper

BREAKFAST IN BED
by Sandra Brown

DON'T TALK TO STRANGERS
by Bethany Campbell

LORD SAVAGE
by Patricia Coughlin

LOVE'S A STAGE
by Sharon and Tom Curtis

DON'T MISS THESE FABULOUS
BANTAM WOMEN'S FICTION TITLES

On Sale in November

AFTER CAROLINE *by Kay Hooper*
"Kay Hooper is a master storyteller." —Tami Hoag

The doctors told Joanna Flynn that she shouldn't suffer any ill effects from her near-fatal accidents, but then the dreams began. Now she must find an explanation, or she'll lose her mind—perhaps even her life.

___09948-5 $21.95/$26.95

BREAKFAST IN BED
by sizzling New York Times bestseller Sandra Brown

Sandra Brown captures the wrenching dilemma of a woman tempted by an unexpected—and forbidden—love in this classic novel, now available in paperback. ___57158-3 $5.50/$7.50

DON'T TALK TO STRANGERS
by national bestseller Bethany Campbell
"A master storyteller of stunning intensity." —Romantic Times

Young women are disappearing after meeting a mysterious stranger on the Internet, and it's Carrie Blue's job to lure the killer . . . without falling prey to his cunningly seductive mind. ___56973-2 $5.50/$7.50

LORD SAVAGE *by the acclaimed Patricia Coughlin*

Ariel Halliday has eight weeks to turn a darkly handsome savage into a proper gentleman. It will take a miracle . . . or maybe just falling in love.

___57520-1 $5.50/$7.50

LOVE'S A STAGE *by Sharon and Tom Curtis*
"Sharon and Tom's talent is immense." —LaVyrle Spencer

Frances Atherton dares to expose the plot that sent her father to prison, but soon she, too, is held captive—by the charms of London's most scandalous playwright and fascinating rake. ___56811-6 $4.99/$6.99
